Alix Nathan was born in London and educated there and at York University where she read English and Music. She now lives in the Welsh Marches where she owns some ancient woodland. She has published many short stories and her novel *The Flight of Sarah Battle* will come out with Parthian in 2015. She has recently completed another novel, *Into the Depths*.

HIS LAST FIRE

Alix Nathan

Parthian
The Old Surgery
Napier Street
Cardigan
SA43 1ED
www.parthianbooks.com

First published in 2014
© Alix Nathan
All Rights Reserved

ISBN 978-1-908946-31-7

The publisher acknowledges the financial support
of the Welsh Books Council.

Edited by Claire Houguez

Cover design by Claire Houguez
and www.theundercard.co.uk

Typesetting by Claire Houguez

Printed and bound by Gwasg Gomer, Llandysul, Wales

British Library Cataloguing in Publication Data

A cataloguing record for this book is available from the
British Library.

HIS LAST FIRE

For N

Contents

His Last Fire

1

The Play's the Thing

9

Flask Between the Lips

15

Revolutionary

19

Shell:
The Pedlar's Tale

27

Shell:
The Sailor's Tale

35

Eels

43

Lapland

49

A Tulip Sky

57

What Was Left to Know

63

Spy
69

Lascia ch'io Pianga
77

Mad
85

Forgiven
95

Shriven
105

From the Life
111

An Experiment:
Above
117

An Experiment:
Below
129

No Applause
143

Notes
153

Acknowledgements
157

His Last Fire

When France plunged towards terror in 1789 England looked on amazed, apalled. Enlightened England! Among the criminals executed before the debtors' door at Newgate that March was a woman condemned for coining. The men were hanged, the woman burned at the stake. Jack was ten, a shrimp of a lad. His father drifted along with the crowds and seeing little in the crush, sat Jack upon his shoulders to report and learn the consequences of wrong-doing.

Pinned by his father's hard grip on his legs he watched the shrieking woman in her coarse gown hustled onto the pyre. Bound, hands, feet and neck, her shuddering moans were suddenly strangled into silence as the stool was snatched from under her. The neatly constructed pile of faggots lit with ceremony soon caught, but Jack longed for the fire to blaze up faster, to roar and consume that terrible, contorted face so that he would no longer have to see it. He willed the flames to rise, to burn, to purge, as he'd willed them ever since.

Now, the century's wheel having turned, he made a good if erratic living. There was danger, though no more than most endured, except the rich. His method was foolproof. He would find the weakness, the Achilles heel of a building: a mass of wormy wood in the structure, glass that would burst in heat, hay in an attached coach house. He'd call at the back gate, Lieutenant Tom Carlisle, wounded at Cape St Vincent, be admitted from pity and discover places for ignition, ways in and out, who and how many lived there. At night, crutch, bandages, naval coat stowed, he'd return to start the fire. Spark, smoke, gusts of spurting flame. As a youth he'd stolen his father's tinder-box and lit fires in alleys, empty yards, dry ditches. Spark, smoke, spurting flame – the same pattern.

But arson alone is not lucrative. Once a building was alight, he'd sound the alarm as though he'd noticed flames while passing and urgently, gently hand the occupants out into the safety of the street. Brave Jack Cockshutt! Always the last to leave the burning building, he emerged through folds of smoke and flocculating ash, his pockets discreetly filled; for often meanness overcame relief in the size of his reward.

It was easy the night of the great storm. Wary of becoming too familiar in London he set off for Liverpool. It was thunderous June and, before the three-inch hailstones fell, lightning had struck the chimney of an attorney's house in the city, travelling through the attics, shattering a staircase window, along bell-wires into bedrooms and down into the kitchen where the servants cowered. It was simple to enter at the back stairs and pocket a fistful of jewels before pulling the lawyer and his wife, smoking slightly, from their splintered bed.

Later, when the worst was over, he joined them on their knees in the parlour to thank the Lord for sparing them. He thanked a Lord in whom he couldn't believe.

He chose lodgings according to the age and condition of the landlord – the older and drunker the better. A degree of squalor was worth enduring if it ensured less suspicion. Still, Jack kept himself shaved and clean and when not playing the Lieutenant he would stroll the streets like any gentleman of leisure, his bearing fine and upright, his features strong, his countenance open. Back in his room he would look at his face in the glass and wonder.

He never courted a woman, rarely had a drab, for memory always intervened. It was enough to see women smile, to watch their faces relax in relief; to receive a bag of sovereigns from the men. He always left quickly, his desire for escape perceived as modesty.

His biggest blaze was the opera house. He dodged in by a side door and made his way to the highest floor beneath the roof, a kind of gallery above the stage. He climbed over machinery and stared down at dancers practising their steps to a spinet. Like a god he gazed, charmed and alarmed by these women in their rough linen practice jackets. His memory flickered; yet they chattered and pranced without concern.

Around him, among the winding gear, pulleys, handles and wires, lay piles of rubbish, discarded back-cloths, rope, theatre bills and scraps of material. He bundled paper and rags into balls and dipped them in jars of grease near the machinery wheels. He lit two, tossed them toward the musicians' pit, watched them flare. As the music stopped and dancers screamed and fled he lobbed the rest onto the emptying boards and rushed for the stairs. He escorted the last few dancers onto the street and retreated with everyone else to a safe distance.

From where he watched a spectacle of the greatest brilliance. Smoke and flames rose in enormous breaths, exhaling sheets of singed music and ash flakes, and as these dropped about him wine bottles from the cellars exploded into a gorgeous flaming column. He moved back from the heat, transfixed by the luteous, rubescent spiral of flame that lit the still night of London like day, lividly licking church spires, causing the cross on St Pauls to shine out.

But that was of another order. It helped him not a jot towards rent or victuals; instead gave him an artist's pleasure. It was a beautiful thing, wondrous. Nor was he alone in thinking so. He heard the other spectators' remarks and read a fine description in the newspapers. Far grander than the account of the Turkish ambassador's carriage breaking down.

*

This would be his last fire. The girl had taken his heart when he'd believed himself content to live alone. Her sweet upward look as she answered the door to him had loosened his soul.

'Mrs Cantley is busy, but she will surely not object.'

Mrs Cantley was the housekeeper, he supposed. The girl led him along a dark corridor to the kitchen where, mindful of his crutch and bandaged foot, she offered him a stool. She brought tea and a piece of bacon while he made mental notes of doors, locks and stairways.

He told his usual story: victorious advance under Admiral Jervis, shots from the Spanish three-decker, humiliating need to beg from house to house. Her round-faced kindness tempted him to embellish, but he couldn't; he'd rather have minimised the fiction, unburdened himself.

Polly, baptised Mary, had been in service now for eighteen months, since 1807. Yes, she liked the position. Her work was hard but there was plenty to eat, the mistress was fair and she could visit her family once a year.

The room was cavernous; one window barred the light. Yet to him it glowed with her cheerfulness. Her small mouth, making little movements as he spoke, laughed readily. A woman who had not suffered, who would not.

The conversation was prosaic; his feelings soared. He made up his mind: a last fire. He'd lead an honest life – set up as a locksmith – marry Polly, take succour from her happiness. One final fire, to impress her, to gain her.

The house belonged to a chandler rich enough to live some distance from his shop. Jack thought to fire the upper floor of the coach house, close to the back of the main building. He himself would enter through the door Polly had opened to him, its lock being weak, and rescue her either from the kitchen regions where maids sometimes slept or from the attics.

Stars were out; clouds smeared a small moon. He removed a pane and climbed through the window of the stable. The horses stirred; he'd let them out shortly. He pulled himself onto the coach roof and set his tarred rags in between the boards above, which doubled as floor for the hayloft.

He could hear noises overhead from the groom sleeping in the hay and as soon as the rags were alight he ran round with a hayfork. The hayloft door over the street was closed; he reached up with the fork and beat upon it.

It opened a crack.

'Fire!' he called, not too loudly. 'Your hay'll catch. You'd best get out quick.'

'Wait,' said a man's voice, opening the door wide. 'There are two of us here,' and half turning he called urgently into the room.

A figure appeared in the opening, chivvied and pushed towards the edge. Bare legs dangled one side of the iron hay-bale pulley.

'Quickly!' called Jack in the dark, 'I'll catch you.'

'Go on!' The groom gave a shove and a woman, petticoat pulled hastily about her, dropped into Jack's arms.

His soul turned black; seared by recognition.

He thrust her away, ran, released the horses and made for the house, heart pouring misery. He stumbled in the yard and hit his head against the jamb picking the lock of the back door. He'd thought she'd save him from his memory! He'd wanted her to save him from himself. Now she herself would be nothing but a memory: her smile illuminating the dark kitchen, the momentary touch of her nakedness.

A window above burst. The flames were catching. He rushed past kitchen, pantries, storerooms, up into the house. As usual his task was not difficult, for having begun the fire at the back, the main staircase was still untouched. With gallantry exaggerated by anguish he led the master and mistress, querulous in their nightgowns, towards the street door. The rest of the household roused each other, gathering in the hall to be counted.

An old woman, probably Mrs Cantley, hair straggling under her cap, hastened over to the mistress.

'My lady. Polly have run back up. To get her things.'

'Mercy! Sir,' she turned to Jack. 'You are fearless. My youngest maid has put herself in danger. She is a foolish girl, but I wouldn't have her burn. I beg you, help her. We shall reward you, sir.'

The staircase narrowed as he reached the attics. He ran the length of the left passage, hearing, before he saw it, how the well roared as the back stairs were consumed. Nobody would survive that. He turned the other way, calling her name.

He found her in a tiny, windowless room, stuffing belongings into a box.

'You must come, now, Polly. There's no time for those.' He pulled her down the first flight.

'How do you know my name?' she panted by his side. 'Who are you?'

He pulled harder.

'Oh! I know you now. It's no good looking away. I recognise you. You're the officer who came. But you've no crutch, no limp. It was a trick!'

'Quiet! You must come!'

'Where are you taking me? You deceived me. For all I know you set the house alight yourself. To rob. To murder me! Oh, help, help!'

They had reached the grand staircase. Newly bought old masters peered out in the hall; everyone had fled to the street. Smoke from the upper floors rolled down upon them.

He turned her to him, clutched her shoulders, shook her.

'By all that's good, I swear I'm no murderer. I came to save you. If you give me away I shall tell the master and mistress where you were last night. They'll believe me, not you and you'll be out in the cold. You have no choice, Polly. I'm saving your life. Saving you from fire and from penury.

'And for that I must have my reward. For that *you* must save *me*. Only you can. I shall marry you, make a good woman of you, while you make a good man of me. Burn the memory out of my head with the glow of your face.' He held it, smoke-blackened, tear-riven between his hands.

THE PLAY'S THE THING

He fired two slugs and missed. The two he'd cast himself from lead. One went a yard to the left of the king, the other into the next box. For a moment nothing happened. He knew such moments: shot discharged, target pierced, uniform, flesh, bone. The terrible look of dismay.

But not this time. Even as he felt his arms gripped, the pistol wrenched from his hand, a forearm at his windpipe, he saw musicians clamber onto the stage, heard the shrieks 'Seize him!' 'Show him!', saw the king step forward. He swivelled his eyes to the crowd: one great glittering, powdered body, one gaping mouth demanding 'God Save the King!'. Kelly ordered his musicians back into the pit; before the green baize curtain actors and singers sang the turgid tune again and again with an extra verse triumphantly scribbled by Sheridan, perspiring in the glare.

From every latent foe,
From the assassin's blow,
God save the King.

He saw and heard it all. The entire theatre, pit, boxes, galleries galvanised in the blaze of a thousand candles.

*

They pulled him about but found no other weapons, no incriminating papers.

'He's an officer, Mr Addington sir,' said Tamplin from the band, his trumpet laid to one side. 'See his waistcoat buttons.'

Hadfield elbowed him away.

'Mr Addington. Mr Sheridan. Gentlemen. I'll tell you who I am. James Hadfield, Captain, 15th Light Dragoons. I have fought for my king and country.'

'And *against* your king, evidently.'

'It's not over yet.'

There's a great deal more and worse to be done.

'Your meaning?'

All rose at the sudden, scented entrance of the Prince of Wales and Duke of York. Hadfield, already standing, smiled broadly, stepped towards the duke.

'I know your Royal Highness – God bless you! You are a good fellow. I have served with your highness and got these and more than these in fighting by your side.' The deep cut over his eye, the long scar on his cheek.

'I was three hours among the dead in a ditch at Lincelles before the French took me prisoner. Had my arm broken by a shot; eight sabre wounds in my head. But I recovered, and here I am.'

Now I've muddled them. Never could keep quiet, even as a boy. Look at them biting their pens.

'Continue your account, Hadfield.' The soft brogue of Sheridan.

'I was discharged from the army because of my wounds. I've made a good deal of money at my trade – silversmith. But I'm tired, sir.' *Hams aching. Let me sit!*

Addington paused in his writing, squinted, wry, silicious:

'How can you explain your action tonight, Hadfield?'

'May I sit, sir?'

'Not yet.'

'Weary. I'm weary of life.'

Sheridan shifted to the other foot. A yawn bubbled behind his hand.

'Is this your pistol?'

'I bought a pair of pistols yesterday from William Wakelin, St John Street. Hairdresser, broker. He cheated me. One was good for nothing. That's the other. Bought a crown's worth of powder this morning; cast the balls myself. On the way, stopped for a jug at Mrs Mason's, Red Lion Street.'

Oh, Nancy. I should have been back there with you now, triumphant. Out like a bullet through the musicians' door. Down the alleys, darkness. But here I stand before this silk-coated rabble! You never denied me anything, Nancy. Oh, get me out of this mishmash somehow!

'And then?'

'Arrived; took my seat on the benches. Paid for, sir. You know the rest.'

Wigs and periwigs, pomade and powder conferred.

'Captain Hadfield,' began Addington. 'It seems you are a man of honourable military record, successful in your trade, honest in your account of yourself so far. You do not appear to be inebriated. Yet you tell us that you attempted the life of the best of sovereigns because you were *tired*, because you were *weary*?'

'I fired to miss, sir.'

Easier to bag than a pheasant. But I let it fly away.

'I'm as good a shot as any in England. I did not attempt to kill the king. I am weary of life, as I told you.'

A jug'd revive me, though. I'd down it in two minutes straight.

'What induced you to do it?'

'I wished for death, sir.' *His.* 'I wished for death.' *Dissemble, man! Feign!* 'But not by my own hand. I desired to raise an alarm. I wished the spectators might fall upon me.'

Addington sceptical, sharp-nosed:

'Do you belong to the Corresponding Society?'

'Surely it was proscribed, sir?'

'It is I who ask the questions, Captain. *I* am examining *you*. Do you belong to the Corresponding Society?'

'I belong to a club of odd fellows and a benefit society. Mrs Mason's my place, not the Bell.'

He pressed his hand to his heart.

'As God is witness, I had no accomplices.'

You'll not take anyone else. My friends. Companions. Together we've skewered the court, razed Buckingham House, rammed a catapotium down parliament's throat!

But this was my design alone. Prune the tree of Liberty: a log is as good as a king. I boasted, they cheered.

They let him sit to await witnesses who came by the dozen. Wakelin, foppish and sly. Yes, he'd sold Hadfield two pistols. Coke, Harley, Baldwin and Pyke, dear fellows, swearing to his good character. Recalling the evil effects of drink. Shopmates, grimy with silver, testifying to his fine work were it not for the beer. Adjutant and captain from the 15th Light telling of his bravery, how beloved of the regiment, how fierce in his cups. His cut brow frowned.

They wish to help me, but I'll not be held a blear-eyed drunkard.

Mrs Nancy Mason, stately and only a little soiled, strong hands before her, proclaimed her honesty, her knowledge that Captain Hadfield rarely drank more than a jug, that drink never made him incapable. But he would complain of pains in the head.

Oh, how often have I wormed my throbbing skull between your earth-warm breasts, Nancy. Soothed by you. Soothed.

'Not the drink, sir. The wounds do drive him hollow.'

'Hollow, Mrs Mason?'

'He do tell of his head empty and hollow save for the pains. I believe it was the reason they put him in the strait waistcoat when he visited his regiment last year. But he were only bellowing from the cuts. They soon let him out.'

'Though I swear he did speak with a madman last Tuesday, sir. Truelock, cobbler at Islington.'

Good woman! Your wit was ever bright. No fiz-gig, you. That way you'll absolve me and release me when the smoke clears, the fire dies down. I'd not mind a spell in Dr Simmons's madhouse.

Truelock, small, fingers too clean for a fully employed cobbler, fixed an inner gaze on Jesus, soon to visit this world. Yes, he'd spoken to Hadfield and convinced him beyond doubt of the speedy return of Our Saviour. Soon, coming soon, with the birth of the new century.

Chins, curls, cravats consulted. 'Deranged', 'insane', 'lunatic' tottered to and fro among them.

Hadfield, hearing, winked wildly at the impassive Truelock.

For that is how I must play it. Confirm Nancy's 'honesty' and give them the story they seek. Conspiracy and drunkenness won't do; a madman will.

Pyke and I saw Garrick play Hamlet, years back. 'The play's the thing': we bandied that about in the Red Lion. What better place than Drury Lane, I said. Lights, splendour, populace to watch.

Still, Hamlet wanted to catch the king's conscience not kill him. Why didn't Harley pull me up on that? He's our pedant. And when Hamlet did think to kill Claudius it was alone in the dark, not in the glare of a full Theatre Royal.

But no, that's not it. The place was right. I was perfectly positioned in the pit, pistol primed, resolve fortified by friends, cock warmed by Nancy's certain touch. It was my conscience that was caught, sharpened by starving paupers crying for bread in Spitalfields this February. Thrown frost-ruined potatoes by liveried lackeys while the court guzzled beefsteak and creams.

Why then? Why did I miss?

Sitting in the three-shillings, unsuspecting clerks on either side, chatter, instruments tuning, I was calm – not even drops of hot wax on my neck made me flinch. The king arrived. I rose. Levelled. Imagined the bullet entering his jacket, waistcoat, shirt, skin, muscle, heart.

Then saw the snowy-wigged, pink-cheeked face. Gibbous eyes smiling with incomprehension. Madness flitting behind them. How could I shoot such a one?

He rose and shouted: 'God knows of the dreams I've had. I received a great commission in my sleep, gentlemen. I know I'm to be a martyr. I was persecuted by the French and I'm to be persecuted again. I have not yet suffered sufficiently.'

Addington spoke: 'Religiously insane. Take him and Truelock to Cold-bath-fields. I'll write a report for *The Times*: Attempt on the life of the King. His Majesty safe. Madman apprehended.'

Flask Between the Lips

'Maria. Maria! Come immediately!'

Brighthelmstone, 1788. The benefits of sea-water.

During the day Robert carried her to the bathing machine. Most nights she sat up, watching the moonlit sea, listening to waves pounding the garden wall, her beautiful profile framed by a half-open window. The sea inspired her, she said. She wrote reams of poems, distracting herself from pain, humiliation.

That night she'd heard the knocking of a boat against the wall.

'Come, Maria! Come!' The table held pens, paper, letters, laudanum. I tucked a fallen blanket under her lifeless legs and we watched two fishermen beach the boat. From it they carried a man, laid him gently on the stones, wrapped a sail around him, pushed the boat out and rowed away.

'A murder!' she said.

'Hush, Mama. Calm yourself.'

The men returned, dragging sticks and branches from the boat and built a fire. She sucked in her breath.

'Immolation!'

Not so. In the moon's brightness we watched them sit their limp friend up, hold out his hands to the flames, pat his cheeks, push a flask between his lips, fan the heat towards him.

She called to Robert, who came from his loft, tousled, blear-eyed, pulling on his great coat. We saw him run into the garden, spring over the side wall onto the beach as the men rowed off. All he could do was confirm death in the embers' light.

But no one took away the body. No one identified it, buried it. For days bathers came and went, some on their way to the hot and cold baths – *hygea devota*. They stared, threw up their hands, pressed kerchiefs against their faces or walked past, self-absorbed.

She couldn't bear it, she said. Abandoned, unclaimed, she saw the dead sailor as herself, discarded by the world, unjustly treated. When she heard that he could not be buried because he 'didn't belong to the parish', Robert posted up her proposal for a subscription to raise money for burial. When this failed she sent him with a little money to local fishermen who dragged the rotting body to the cliff and covered it with stones. Uncommitted. Unprayed-for.

I remember it. The cold night, spark-shadowed bulk, hopeless acts of revival, the furtive retreat. More, I remember her declarations of tragedy, gestures of indignation, performance of melancholy. The nib scraping new poems onto backs of envelopes.

'Maria, Maria, come quickly!'

Bath was worse, without the virtue of salt breezes. She could not sleep at night after a day of immersion in intolerable heat – how we sweated in our brown linen jackets and petticoats in the sulphurous steam, pushing away the useless floating bowls of pomander – and the water in the Pump Room disgusting to drink. Nor was it better out of the water in the crowds of ogling, hobbling sick. Each day we spent hours on her dress, her hair, in case she should be recognised.

'I need not remind you that Royal Heads have turned, Maria. I shall not lose my looks though I have lost the use of my legs. You may not understand, since you cause no heads to turn, but can at least *imagine*.'

'Maria!' Here in Englefield in our cottage *ornée* old acquaintances still called and for each she would perform tragic beauty or woman of wit, once adored, now maligned. We prepared hair powder, muslins, ribbons, gauze neckerchiefs, caps, books, papers, the Prince's miniature. Alone again, she wrote and wrote, and we posted her collection of poems with the 'Haunted Beach', her 'favourite offspring'.

'I shall never forget that horror,' she said.

There was an accident. One morning, lifted from her bed by Robert, she hit her head badly on the sloping ceiling.

'You *tossed* her?' I asked him later.

'She made a sudden movement. Clutched my arm: "Robert, I *know* . . ." but she never said, you see.'

Towards the end, I slept on a cot in her room. Visitors had become sparse, for few care to enter a sick room, but there were letters by the dozen, providing envelopes on which to write the *Memoirs*. She worried so much about finishing the second half entitled 'Completed by a Friend'.

'For they will think the friend is you, Maria, and what better advocate for a wronged woman than her innocent daughter?' I shrank from her look.

And now she's dead, the final, gruelling dropsy over. How often I held her to help her breathe, counted out the drops of laudanum, wiped her, cleaned her, brushed back her damp hair. Had she done the same for me? The *Memoirs* tell me nothing of my life except where, as a baby, I helped entrance Mr Sheridan. I remember only nurses. Names, places, dresses, poems, a life of beauty, fame and injustice in which I played almost no part; a passing reference. Did Godwin notice me, or Pindar, when they, two lone mourners, came to walk the coffin to its grave?

In 1788 I was fourteen, no longer a child, useful at last. For twelve years I have tended, nursed, accompanied, approved, averted my gaze, kept the tradesmen from the door. Over the Channel they lit their flare for Liberty until it died, blackened beyond recognition. I, too, needed my revolt.

Robert Sanders, footman, groom, obliged to buy his own boots, who carried her countless times from bed to chair to commode to couch to carriage, up stairs, down, day and night. I remember that night in Brighthelmstone. For in the corridor leading to the pantry Robert held me in his arms. His great coat smelled of sea and burnt branches.

Yesterday he said: 'I have carried her that often I know the feel of her body better than I know yours. That shouldn't be.'

We declared our love for each other an age ago. At last we can marry, live here. The cottage is mine – it's all I have – and Robert can find employment nearby. Our expenses would be few for we'd see no one.

Or I could attend the voice, still sounding, that would tolerate no scandal but her own.

'Maria! Come immediately!'

Live alone, write begging letters, publish the *Memoirs*. Live alone, hold up the image of my famous mother for whom Royal Heads turned, pat its cheeks, draw its hands to the flames. Push a flask between its lips, fan the hopeless heat towards it.

Revolutionary

The boy's throw was accurate. The gulls were quicker of course; like crows they sensed hostility before it struck. If he sat next to the boy nobody would look twice seeing two anonymous backs along the quay. Not that they'd think to come here. Wrong side of the river. They'd start with Hardman, obviously, his partner in law. Pick up on the copemen in Tooley street and the light-horsemen – but they were far too canny to be caught.

The bills of lading game was shot. He'd have to clear off soon. Get right away. Try something else.

He was out of breath after his brisk walk over the bridge, along Tower Street, down Beer Lane. The boy's legs hung over the slimy stone, a pile of chippings on the ground next to him.

'You're good at it,' said William Leopard. 'Ever tried a pistol?'

The boy looked up, startled. Leopard noted: clean, well-fed, sensitive, self-absorbed. About fifteen.

'Shouldn't you be in school?' Still no reply.

'William Leopard,' he extended his hand though it wasn't taken. 'May I sit here with you?'

'As you wish,' the boy growled, voice new-broken. 'Shouldn't *you* be at work?'

'Good question!' Leopard laughed. 'Give me one of your stones, will you?'

Before them were barges lashed together three deep, stretched six along. Wooden chests marked B E N G A L. So easy for scuffle-hunters! Perhaps straight theft was better than false papers. Damned bad luck. But he wouldn't stoop to jemmies and night work.

Gulls stood in a row on the outer edge of the barges, flew up, screaming, dived and fought for booty, returned to the row again. Leopard aimed, missed. As he expected, the boy picked a missile, lined up and drove a bird, screeching, into the air.

'Bulls-eye! What did you say your name was?'

'I didn't. Matthew Dale.'

'Matt?'

'Matthew.'

'Shouldn't you be a little further up, Matthew, fishing from Dice Quay?'

'Can't take fish home.'

'Oh?'

'As you said, I'm supposed to be at school.'

'And which school is that?'

But the boy wasn't going to tell him, just as he, too, would keep certain facts to himself.

'What is *your* work?' the boy asked Leopard suddenly, plucking at erratic courage.

He looked at the man and found him extraordinary. His clothes were dusty, grimy, stained yet made from good cloth. He was educated too, as well as prying. Must be cautious, couldn't have the man report him. Yet he didn't look the reporting type. Too unshaven and amused.

'The law,' said Leopard. 'I'm a lawyer. Doing a little business.'

'*Here*?'

'A somewhat difficult transaction, you know. Merchants need me in these parts.' He waved his hand vaguely.

'Oh.'

'Sugar, brandy, wheat. There's 77,000 tons of iron due from Petersburg,' he sighed.

Matthew yawned.

'I see you're not interested in trade, young man.'

'No.'

'You're a revolutionary! A *Jacobin* – that's what you are.'

The boy blushed. His features were delicate; bore the burden of transition, of daring in conflict with caution.

'You hate this corrupt world, this vicious self-seeking government.'

Matthew hunched himself. The man was laughing at him. Any minute now he'd reveal himself as an unusual friend of his father's and trudge him back home.

'I'm serious, young man. *I* hate this corrupt world, this vicious self-seeking government.'

'Then why do you work in it?'

'Good question! Have you read Tom Paine?'

He wished the man would go. He knew they'd find out sooner or later and beat him, but later was what he hoped for. He was here because he hated company. He wished the man would go.

'Look!' Leopard rummaged in his bulging pockets and pulled out a book. Thumbed, greasy. *Rights of Man, vol. I.* 'Have you read it?'

'It's banned,' Matthew said. Embarrassed at the folly of this remark he stuttered: '*And* I've read *volume II.*'

'I knew it! A man after my own heart. Shake hands, citizen!'

The gulls flew up at this burst of activity and noise from the quay.

'What a great book it is! Who has done more for the world than he? But it's no good reading banned books behind closed shutters, is it? You're still too young for action, I suppose. Sitting on the quayside's not going to help the world.'

'*You're* sitting on the quayside, too.'

'Yes, yes, *now* I am. And no doubt dodging school is a start. What is your father?'

Matthew mumbled.

'A *chaplain*! A man of the cloth! Oh Lord! Then I admire you, Matthew. You defy your school, you defy your father. I myself shall go to America.'

'Ah!' The boy sat back and stared at this surprising companion with the blackguardly face. Bulbous nose, lank hair, black, all-seeing eyes.

'France was the place, as you know. But the French have defiled themselves, betrayed their principles. They have not drowned corruption in the blood they've spilled; it has welled up again. America is the only place to be. Paine knows that himself.

'But you have made a beginning, young Matthew. Already you are countering authority – is there not something even bolder you can do?'

'Perhaps.' As he hesitated an idea formed. 'Tomorrow. I think I can do something revolutionary by then. Will you come again tomorrow?'

'Well. Yes, young man. I could do that. I need some time to make arrangements. But maybe we should meet somewhere else. Mustn't arouse suspicion. These new river police are on the prowl looking for men with hogsheads stuffed down their trousers.' He laughed immoderately. 'How about the beach below the Tower?'

'*No!* Here's better. There's nobody about, is there?'

'Well, here then. But look. *Should* anyone ask for me, you haven't seen me. Have no notion who they're talking about. Nobody of my description. *Could* you describe me?'

'I think I could.'

'Well don't. And *I* haven't seen *you*. Truant? Never met one! Agreed?'

They shook hands. 'Porters' Quay, eight o'clock!'

Matthew watched the insolent set of Leopard's shoulders as he walked briskly up the street. He turned back to the river. He couldn't go home for hours yet.

It was clear and hot soon after daybreak. The river was thick with boats. Barges formed an inner margin below quays and wharves. Dredgers, lighters, floating fire engines waited. Mid-stream lay masted ships, sails half-furled, brigs, cutters, West Indiamen, their cargoes unloaded by lightermen. Over the rest of the water darted skiffs and rowing boats, sculled, punted, fishing, scouting, ferrying.

Matthew paced the quay. Smiles broke on his taut face. Leopard was late and he could hardly bear the wait.

At last the man arrived, walking rapidly. They shook hands. Matthew noticed that Leopard wore exactly the same clothes. A strong sourness suggested he'd slept in them.

'Citizen Dale! Did anyone look for me? No sniffing quay guards?'

'No, Citizen Leopard. Not a soul.'

'That's a relief. But let me warn you, Matthew, I am a little jumpy today.'

'Oh?'

'My business has not gone well. But now, let me see. No one found *you* out, either, then? Your parents do not suspect?'

'So far not. But have you forgotten, Mr Leopard? Have you forgotten my revolutionary act?'

'Ah! No, goodness no! What have you done, citizen?'

'I wish you to guess.'

'How can I do that? I hardly know you.' He looked round about him and back to Matthew impatiently.

'What I have done can be seen,' said Matthew proudly. 'It can be seen from *here*.'

'From *here*! Well! In that direction ships, more ships, London Bridge, waterworks, Hanks' timber, Fowler's, Clove's.' He tailed off. Must he play *games* for this final 'transaction'?

'Wrong direction.'

'Behind me?'

'No.'

'That leaves the river, barges, ships; they all look the same to me; wharves warehouses on the other side, or to the left,' he swung round slowly, 'the walls of the Tower.'

'The Royal Arms are flying,' said Matthew, 'for it's the King's birthday today. June 4th.'

They both looked towards the White Tower.

'Good God! Do my eyes deceive me? Did *you* do that? *Did* you? The work of a genius! Citizen Dale!'

From the ramparts of the White Tower protruded a second flagpole and from that flagpole in the glory of the June morning, flew the Tricolor.

'Did you do that?'

'Yes.'

'But how? How on earth?'

'My father is deputy chaplain of the Tower,' said the boy both ashamed and proud.

'You *live* there then!'

'Yes.'

'Is it true there are apple trees in the grounds?'

24

'Yes. But what of that? I was up early. No one saw me – not even the lions in the menagerie. And *still* no one has noticed else it would have been struck by now.'

'Where did you *find* a Tricolor?'

'We made it. My sister and I. We sewed it last night from pieces of silk we found.'

'So, you're not in this alone. Did you tell her about me?'

'No. But in any case, Sophie will not tell. Nor shall I tell of *her* when I am found out.'

'Then you had better not return. And I . . .'

They were stopped by an immense booming.

'It's not the powder mills exploding!' shouted Matthew, for Leopard had nearly jumped out of his skin. Cannon were firing from St James's and suddenly, very close, were answered by those at the Tower.

'It's for the King. Yet my flag still flies!' The boy laughed like a child.

'Matthew. Tomorrow I take a ship to America. To freedom. The only land in the world where liberty, equality and fraternity truly live – better by far than your French. No, don't be downcast. The flag's a grand gesture. You have proved yourself.'

Leopard paced around the boy with tense steps.

'Come to America with me! *I* shall escape my little trouble here and *you* will escape punishment. For what will they do when they find that it was you?'

The boy's delight had gone. He watched the sharp eyes darting like flies.

'Yes, come with me. We can meet here tomorrow before the sailing. It had better be nine o'clock, in time for the tide. Bring as many clothes as you can fit in a single bundle. I believe the winters are cold there. And bring as much money as you can. For your passage.'

'I shall have to steal it.'

'Is stealing worse than hoisting the flag of the enemy on the King's Birthday? We are at war with France! That's *treason*!

'Now Matthew, think only of America. Your future lies *there*. The ship sails to Philadelphia. I shall find work as a lawyer and you, with your schooling, there'll be all manner of opportunities. And women, Matthew! There's women aplenty in the land of liberty!'

The boy looked down. Leopard glanced about him again.

'Come, Matthew. Let us shake hands on it. If I'd a bottle we could toast ourselves. To America! Till tomorrow!'

And he was gone with his rapid steps. Along stones still black from the stream of liquid fire when the sugar warehouse went up. Matthew felt utterly dejected and excited beyond anything he'd ever known before. America. Freedom.

He looked up. The Tricolor had gone.

June 5th was hot again. A burning sky dried the sludge at low tide, magnified the stink of fish and sewage. The upper air was clear, the lower dense with steam and smoke, hops, malt, pitch. There was little activity on the river, the barges beached, boats bobbing only in mid-stream. The gulls at Porters' Quay had flown up river to Fishmonger's Hall to await the flounders and smelt, shad, lampreys, jack, perch, chub.

The tide returned, boats breathed, ships shifted. Satiated, the gulls swooped back to their spattered row on the barges knocking against the stone. The boxes from B E N G A L had not been unloaded. Porters' quay was deserted. No one came all day.

SHELL: THE PEDLAR'S TALE

Nancy Mason took no excuse from the kitchen, threw out drinkers with the wrong opinions but couldn't resist trinkets, gewgaws, cloth. Beggars were turned away, even sailors wounded by the French, but pedlars never.

She eyed him quickly – not a trouble-maker – and ran her hand over the goods spread on the table. Ribbons, pretty fragments of lace, useful squares of muslin and calico, baubles, buttons of wood, bone, mother-of-pearl, pins, pincushions, thimbles.

'They're good quality,' the pedlar said. Nancy was too shrewd to agree. She picked out some pearl buttons.

'How much for these?'

He assessed her with dully glittering eyes.

'I'll level with you, Ma'am. I'm looking for lodging. Will they pay for a week?'

Nancy rarely troubled to rent out rooms. It was enough keeping the casks rolling in, maintaining a supply of pies. But to have that collection of delights under her roof was irresistible. Besides, she reasoned, the man was gentle, quiet, even fair of face. Must have come down in the world.

She saw little of him, hadn't expected to, but soon Betsy told her he'd taken no food, not left his room for three days. Then she reported him feverish and coughing badly.

Betsy was fourteen, of little experience; the man was probably drunk. Nancy went up to the third floor by the back stairs. She noted his tray of goods on the chest, hat and clothes folded on a chair, water in the basin. He was in bed, yet not unshaven, smelling little, apologetic. She sent for leeches but he only worsened. She called in surgeon Pyke, one of the radicals who met to drink here in her house in Red Lion Street.

'Take goods to pay,' gasped the pedlar, anhelous; still nameless. Nancy chose two squares of lace.

Before Pyke's second visit the pedlar became agitated. Nancy had taken to bathing his fine brow, burning from fever – Betsy was useless – even combing his long hair with one of his own bone combs.

'I'd rather Mr Pyke came no more, Ma'am.'

'He must. I'll not have you die.'

Pyke approached her later.

'Here's a surprise, Mrs Mason. Your pedlar is a woman.'

*

Nancy was handsome, stately. As a young girl, impatient with her origins, she'd gone to London where, from the inevitable but superior whorehouse she made her way to the stage. So many had achieved success – think of Perdita Robinson! Here were the attractions of wonderful cloth: satins, sprigged muslin, gauze, of breeches and sweeping velvet cloaks, boxes of glass and paste jewels. She played minor parts. It was not applause but impersonation that suited the country girl newly launched in town; ladies' maids, fairies, minor goddesses, any part to play but herself.

She became mistress of a worthless baronet for six months then kept house for an ageing merchant. Three children had not survived birth, two sons grown and departed. When the merchant died, leaving his property and name to her, though they'd never married, she opened the house, served good ale, allowed no gaming and no anti-Jacobins. She could tell a government spy before he'd even walked through the door, and although her acting days were done she bluffed with conviction when quizzed. Her customers were men of radical opinion, some more, some less educated, but all touched with the energy of rebellion. She cheered them with her common sense and unexpected wit; listened to their talk, warmed to the heat of their feelings, the colour of their language. And James Hadfield, the warmest of them all, she took to her bed.

'I feared hanging,' the pedlar woman said, when, after a time, Nancy questioned her. At first she'd merely calmed the woman and tended her as Pyke's treatment took effect, practising gentleness unused since her children were at home. Against a backdrop of ribaldry about the woman in breeches, an affection grew between them, until Nancy at last dared to satisfy her curiosity.

It was the Popery seventeen years ago, said the woman, giving her only name as Ellen. She'd got mixed up in Lord Gordon's riots in the summer of 1780.

'They said the king was in danger from papists. We went to defend him. My husband George took me.

'But there were those that rampaged. Attacked buildings. We watched them. We heard the muskets, saw bodies, stepped over them, ran for our lives.'

'And then?'

'They said it wasn't safe to go home. The soldiers knew people from our street took part. We'd be hanged for riot. Some were. They said to go out of the city or hide or disguise oneself. I changed clothes with George. We went different ways.'

Pyke had advised against mental over-exertion. Ellen's tale was long. Nancy, though drawn like a bee to nectar, drank each measure slowly.

'I met some pedlars. Learned where to get goods; to judge which houses were welcoming, which to avoid. Being a pedlar I could move away quickly if anyone suspected me.

'I flattened my breasts with a bandage. Kept to myself during the bleeding, but after a while it stopped. I grew to like men's clothes,' she said. Her voice reduced to a whisp again, her smile shadowed.

'And George?'

'I never saw him. Someone said he'd died.'

Nancy thrilled to the story, its drama, its squalor, even to the royalism she would normally reject. How fat and comfortable her own life seemed against Ellen's perpetual disguise. It was better than the stage, this extraordinary act. Ellen told how at first she slept under hedges, washed in dewponds, bedded down by the ashes of cold ovens; of kindly scullions, heartless children with stones. Perfecting her role, she drank more ale than she could hold, took to a pipe, brawled at cock-fights. Hovered outside a whorehouse. Gradually she made money, bought a horse and cart, rented lodgings. And now she'd returned to London.

'You need play the part no more,' said Nancy. 'The spies are after them as speaks against the war. They've no interest in you. No one remembers those riots, I'm sure. You can be a woman again. I'll find you a gown – cut it to size.'

On the day Nancy gave Betsy the pedlar garments to burn, she helped Ellen from the bed, laying clothes out for her. Glimpsed thin limbs, withered breasts, translucence of old age; knew her to be thirty-eight.

Ellen offered her goods, no longer irresistible glitter to Nancy, but mute companions of her new-found friend's hard life. She took a yard of printed Irish muslin, some pale lilac ribbon. And a silver walnut. It was lighter than it looked, a real walnut shell painted to seem metallic. She pushed a tiny catch and it opened on a minute hinge, revealing miniatures of the king and queen in delicate blue, white and pink brushstrokes, one in each half.

She tucked the walnut in her pocket. How the men downstairs would sneer at the royal portraits if they knew, obsessed as they were with revolution! Often she fingered its smooth fragility.

Nancy had always preferred men to women. Men had provided her living; all her children had been male. She'd escaped her mother as soon as she could. Women were only ever competition or reluctant servants. Ellen broke this rule. Nancy felt fondness as for a precious thing, strange, frangible, uniquely her own. She gave Ellen a better room, retrieved gowns packed away in presses and refashioned them; was glad to pay Pyke for his medicaments. She fed her small delicacies – brandy creams, ratafias, oysters – hoping she'd put on flesh, find lost radiance. She longed to show off her treasure to Hadfield, Coke, Harley and the other men whose fancies sometimes led to danger, but knew their tolerance evaporated with each jug of ale. She kept her to herself.

Yet something eluded Nancy. Of course Ellen had changed herself utterly to save her life. She had become adept at walking and holding herself like a man. She didn't find it easy being a woman again after all this time; gown, cap and shawl seemed merely fresh disguise. Although Nancy had seen her at her weakest, the lines of her face were hard, closed.

Pyke warned Nancy the consumption would prevail. When Ellen wanted to take to the streets once more Nancy tried to prevent her.

'What need have you? Stay here; get well.'

'You are kind. I saw you were when I first came.'

'You chose my house.'

'The streets were so crowded that day.'

'Victory celebrations.' How the men had railed that night!

'But I must go out again.'

'You're not well enough. Stay. Be like a daughter to me.'

The hardness cracked, broke open.

'I cannot. I must find him. My son.'

'You've a *child*?'

'I told you only part. George and I changed clothes. Hid in the burnt out ropemaker's by Stepney causeway. After three days I went home to my child. John. I'd left him with my neighbour. But when I returned no one was there. Not George nor John nor my neighbour. Nobody.'

Here was the core, the kernel.

'People said my neighbour'd been arrested and John taken away for safety. I went to my sister but she didn't have him and George had no family. Nobody knew. I dared not ask at Newgate lest they arrest me. Nor at Coram's.

'In man's clothes I could seek him freely. I asked as I went from house to house. Perhaps he'd been taken in by someone kind. When I heard nothing, I moved on. Found new suppliers, tried different directions. I've searched for seventeen years.'

Pity welled. For Ellen. For herself. Ellen was no longer hers. Never had been.

'Sometimes there was hope. I heard of a boy who was dumb. They said his parents died when he was very young. He was stunned in a fight, suddenly began to speak. I went to look but it wasn't him.

'I asked gypsies. They were not friendly to me, being rivals in trade. I watched children come out of school, stared

32

at every urchin, asked sweeps, tinkers. He'll be twenty years old now. How shall I know him?'

Her eyes darkened, hollowed. Nancy's loss was as nothing.

*

She filled two drawers with Ellen's goods. Felt a remembered pleasure, but neither used the cloth to make kerchiefs nor trimmed her hats with ribbon. Nor did she take up the search for John, since Ellen never gave her surname and nothing among her belongings revealed it.

Nancy had grasped a passing friendship. Held it fast while she could. It consoled her that Ellen had chosen Red Lion Street in which to die. She would never care for another woman as, momentarily, she'd cared for Ellen.

From time to time she held the walnut in her hands, registered its surprising lightness, opened the tiny clasp, admired the almost invisible brushstrokes, wondered at the bland painted faces. She kept it from Hadfield, who would have stamped it underfoot as a piece of royalist trash. Not that she didn't share the views of the man with whom she shared her bed. But Ellen's was a loss no man could comprehend, futile, fatal: she'd lived half her life disguised, dried out, empty.

Nancy touched her shell, her *memento mori*, as she chivvied the maids and cheered the drinkers, balanced the accounts and dragged the boots off her inebriated lover.

SHELL: THE SAILOR'S TALE

Wagons draped with captured colours, French, Spanish, Dutch; naval lieutenants on foot, marines playing; carriages of admirals, the commons, speaker, mace-bearer, clerks of the crown, masters in chancery, judges, peers, Lord High Chancellor. King's household, Queen's, the princesses, three dukes; twenty carriages of state drawn by one hundred and twenty-two horses. To St Paul's to thank God for victory. December clear and bright.

Behind lines of foot guards, horse, city militia, East India volunteers, pushing crowds, curious, impertinent.

Gallant British tars escort the flags. From the *Ardent* that had fought more bravely, lost more men in the fury of Camperdown than any other ship, John Airey. Newly-promoted. Reluctant, tossed on a cross-stream. This day will mark the end, William Leopard instructed him. Come the new year you and I shall sail to America and liberty.

William was older than John, recalcitrant, called the battle shameful. But he hadn't been there. Numberless seamen, the captain and master died as they broke the Dutch line, shattered their vessels. John, exhausted, smoke-smothered, pitch flaming beneath his feet, had stepped over the dead gunner's mate to take his place. A torn spar fell, missing him. Crushing the mate's already crushed body. Unlike his friend, John cannot dismiss these events. Yet neither does he feel pride. He tries not to think.

There'd been few prospects for a young man with a little education, attached to bleak East seascapes. He'd been adopted at three by a childless surgeon whose sickly wife died soon after. His own origins were obscure – he'd only a shadowed memory of his mother – his parents 'lost' during a disturbance in London. A friend of a neighbour with whom he'd been left took him to her home village in Suffolk, where the surgeon also lived. No one would explain what happened. Perhaps they didn't know. He'd wondered if his parents' end had been ignominious; never dared ask.

After his wife died the melancholy surgeon employed an old woman to run his modest household and later a girl, Margaret, a seaman's daughter. Growing into manhood, John perceived the changed relationship between Margaret and his adoptive father almost before it began. His heightened awareness charted the infants she lost, the gradual souring of her expression, just as she became the object of his own desire.

The surgeon was often away; John, fair of face, unclouded, was five years Margaret's junior, not thirty years her senior. For a few months he found tenderness, eased her irritability, caused her to think of smiling. But it was a small house and such pleasure requires privacy. They were soon found out.

John acknowledged that his conduct was a poor return for his upbringing. He became a quota-man, taking the offer of £30 to join the navy. The surgeon stepped up his intake of laudanum, dwindled gradually into blackness. Margaret cast her eyes downward, the lines round her mouth set; she began to resemble the surgeon's childless wife.

John was quick; learned the work of an ordinary seaman easily on his first ship in Lowestoft. Before long he was promoted Able Seaman Airey, assigned to the *Mars* at Spithead. Strong enough to take grog without becoming drunk, obedient yet articulate, he was an obvious choice for seamen's delegate when mutiny blew through the fleet like a sudden squall.

At first it was a mere cry, polite, respectful. They asked for little enough: increased wages, unchanged for a hundred years; sixteen ounces in the pound not fourteen; improved provisions, vegetables instead of flour; sick seamen better attended, paid until well; grievances against officers looked to; leave to go on shore.

The Admiralty was silent. Then came an order to sail: the petitions, one from each ship, ignored.

The *Queen Charlotte* sent a signal to the rest: three cheers hailed from fore-shroud to fore-shroud, defiance ringing out in Sunday sunshine. A line of small boats toured the fleet to the sound of the Easter service.

They formed a General Assembly, two men from each ship. John Airey and William Leopard the *Mars*'s delegates. Like John, William was a quota-man, though for quite different reasons. John's crime had been ingratitude; he joined the navy from remorse. William, a lawyer charged with fraud, took the £30 bounty in place of prison. John was in awe of him, his education, his appearance. He resembled Charles Fox, a rough engraving of whom he kept in his bulging blue jacket, along with pamphlets and both volumes of *The Rights of Man*. Short, stubby, lank black hair. Erratically shaven, clothes filthy, he risked a flogging each time he outwitted a critical officer. The friendship with John was unbalanced, yet teachers need pupils. They rowed to the Assembly in mutual pride.

Thirty-two delegates sat at the table in the *Charlotte*'s state cabin. None was more than forty, some looked much older. John, the youngest at twenty, gleamed with rare freshness. Able seamen, midshipmen, petty officers, a handful of Irish. Between them enough sense to let nothing slip, enough schooling to write letters and petitions to impress narrow-minded superiors. William had legal knowledge, John a neat hand.

All turned to Valentine Joyce. Small, non-descript, Quartermaster's Mate, he quivered with energy, listened with intensity, impatience. Bit his nails till the finger-stumps bled.

'We have no hope of success unless our behaviour is impeccable,' he said.

Strict rules and punishments: ropes hung from every yard-arm as a warning. No liquor on board, no drunkenness, leave or letters. Women who came not allowed off. All should swear an oath 'by his Maker that the cause we have undertaken be persevered in till accomplished.'

'And if the French appear?'

'We sail, of course!'

William grunted behind his hand at this patriotism.

Absolute authority of men over men exhilarated John, but hung like a weight. He was honoured, apalled. William had no time for such scruples. Though they ribbed John for his youth the crew approved of him. He'd known little emotion in his childhood. He and Margaret made no declarations before he went to sea. Some months ago, he'd heard his adoptive father had died: it barely touched him. The cheer of hardened tars sustained him.

The Admiralty, habit-blinkered, could not conceive of rationality in the ranks. Saw only indiscipline, offered small increases in pay, ignored the other requests. Promised forgiveness for immediate return to duty.

'Why trust them?' William challenged Joyce. 'They'll promise us pardon and hang us.'

They argued through the night. Timorous, bold, embittered; midshipmen wary of men and superiors alike; quartermasters, gunners, iron yet loyal, lashed by the revolutionary tongue of William and his Irish cronies. Motley, united by nothing except grievance they were moulded into order and consensus by Joyce, exuding certainty to make all opposition crumble.

'Only the King's pardon will do. No return.'

On his ship *Royal Sovereign* Admiral Gardner, incensed, grey eyes staring, colour rising, faced the assembled crew.

'Damned mutinous blackguards! They know the French are nearby at sea but are afraid of meeting them. Skulking fellows!' He seized a delegate, shook him violently, threatened to shoot him and every fifth man.

Uproar. Hissing riot of men surrounded the blue and gold uniforms, hustled them, sweating, off the ship. Captains throughout the fleet were confined in their cabins.

'We must conduct ourselves wisely,' Joyce warned. 'Only an Act of Parliament will make sure of our demands.'

Once more a missive of remarkable restraint and precision was composed, while feelings round the table broke.

'Would I dearly thrust a dish of burgoo in their faces!'

'Let them crack their teeth on salt horse!' Years old, shrunken, wood-hard.

'Pick out the red worms from cheese!'

'We must be prudent, decent. The people are with us, remember. Look how they line the quays and beach.'

'They should hear what we endure,' cried the *Glory*'s delegate.

John knew of the sufferings, of men who'd rather hurl themselves overboard than die from flogging with a knotted rope's end. The captain who cried: 'I'll see the man's backbone, by God!' He'd read the desperate letter from the *Amphitrite* begging for removal of their first lieutenant, *a most Cruel and Barberous man, Beating some at times untill they are not able to stand, and not allowing them the satisfaction to cry out.*

His heart expanded. And all the while William fed him radical honey, tempted him with Liberty and Equality.

St George's day announced the King's pardon, increase of pay and provisions. Celebrations in Portsmouth. Celebrations on board. Yet the government was in no hurry; soon rumour said the Seamen's Bill would be thrown out.

'They mean to lull us into a supposed state of security.'

'If once they divide us ...'

Finally, bloodshed: a foolhardy officer, a determined admiral, eight hundred enraged men. Brief exchange of fire, men wounded, killed, defeat for the admiral. Red flags flying. Yet the men's revenge for their dead was stillborn, held back by the extraordinary power of Joyce. By respect for hierarchy entangled in their bones like weed.

William despaired.

'The English haven't the blood and guts for revolution.' The Irish delegates murmured agreement. 'There's no hope but America.'

In the end the victory was the men's. Admiral Lord Howe, loved by the Fleet as Black Dick, was dragged from retirement to placate and calm. Weary with age and gout he was rowed from ship to ship, lifted in and out, off and onto ladders to explain and persuade in language that rambled, bored. More pay, better rations, leave and grievances attended to. No one punished for mutiny. The country was contented and the seamen nearly burst their sides with loyalty.

William refused to attend the delegates' celebration dinner. John went, enjoyed himself, knew William was right. In time he was mustered to the *Ardent* in Admiral Duncan's

North Sea fleet. Without the mutiny he became a mere sailor, passive, mindless. Avoided death by chance not choice.

And now, as he enters St Paul's behind the savaged flag of the Dutch fleet, he is lost in colossal space, somehow more vast than open sky, oppressed by the banks of grandeur around him.

'What do they know?' he thinks, touching *vol. II* of Tom Paine that William had thrust in his pocket before he left for London.

'It's their victory, not ours,' William had said. 'The French have failed, corrupted. The only hope is to start afresh on the other side of the Atlantic.'

The ceremony over, John strides away through the city. The militia have dispersed. Shops are closed, crowds spread about the streets in raucous merriment.

In the shadows of Red Lion Street he sees a pedlar peer up into each face that passes. For a moment he imagines buying a keepsake, perhaps a painted seashell, for a red-cheeked, smiling mother who's cared for him all his life.

'I bought this for you in London after the celebration.' She'll keep it on a little table next to her chair by the window, where she looks out to sea with searching eyes.

'My son was at Camperdown,' she'll say and be proud.

He walks on. Into the light of Holborn. No, not America. He'll return to the sweet bleakness of the East coast; make a home with Margaret.

EELS

He called for eels.

She came immediately. 'How do you want them?'

'Pie, with currants. Or pitch-cock. Stewing takes too long.'

'Nutmeg, Jamaica pepper.'

'Just how I like it, Elizabeth. Ah – she is alone the Arabian bird.'

'Cruel! To remind me of my one night as Imogen.'

'… the gods made you

Unlike all others, chaffless!'

She banged the door on his croak of a laugh, the famous hoarse voice. Yet he loved her as well as needed her. He'd always needed women, loved the ones he had. Two wives and now the girl. Richard Yates, comic actor, unequalled as Shakespeare's clowns. 1796, his ninetieth year, loved a girl of twenty-seven. And why not?

He thought with greed about eels. Stewed needed good gravy: claret, anchovy, lemon-peel; collared was for big conger, fennel. She could broil them with butter and oyster pickle but best would be pie, snuggling in hot butter paste. He'd remind her of the cockney in *Lear* putting eels in the pie alive: 'she knapped 'em o' the coxcombs with a stick, and cried 'Down, wantons, down!' She wouldn't laugh.

He picked his long handsome nose. Though short he was lean, remarkably fit, Cruickshank said. Still some teeth; hair thin beneath the wig. But he knew she longed for a young body fresh as a daisy. Not that she was unkind. She feigned.

He had been good to her. Took her in after the fire at the opera house in her rough linen practice jacket; flattered her shallow talent; arranged her one appearance in *Cymbeline*; paid her well as housekeeper. Willed her the house, joking of his 'manacle of love'. It was only right he should ask for a little pleasure. That she dance with him when he was lively, felt a Harlequin coming on, he'd say. He could still step, if not so fine, so fast. That she warm his bed. King Yates. Down, wanton, down. Her hands like hot butter paste.

He dozed. Dreamed he was Fielding's miser Lovegold. How they'd applauded!

'In short, Lappet, I must touch, touch, touch something real.' He'd fondled the word 'touch', raising its temperature to an unexpected explosion of feeling. How they'd roared!

Touch, touch. Real. Eels. Woke at her arrival.

'No eels, Richard. None. I've bought you a flounder.'

'*What?*'

'He'd none left.'

'No *eels*? What could be easier this time of year? The river's stuffed with 'em from Hammersmith to Kew. I've not asked for sea-fish.' He pulled her sleeve, gripped her wrist.

'Sit on my knee, you fair hot wench in flame-coloured taffeta.'

'I'm not hot, Richard, and I'm wearing blue as you can

44

well see. There were no eels. You needs must eat flounder or else cold beef for dinner.'

'Cold wench in blue silk. I'll have eels!'

'He said the catch was small; they sold instantly.'

'Whoreson caterpillar! Bacon-fed knave! Reasons as plenty as blackberries.'

'Calm yourself. Your face is turning red. I met Thomas. Your nephew, Lieutenant Thomas Yates. Waiting outside the house again. He always tells me of his five children, the baby on the way. He disturbs me, Richard.'

'A poor tale.'

'Your brother's son. Great nephews, nieces.'

'I won't have brats running about the house.'

'He's hard-pressed.'

'So he tells you. An officer in the royal navy is paid, you know. I played my patriotic part in '61. Wrote plays, Elizabeth. *The British Tar's Triumph over M. Soupe-Maigre.* Here's the manuscript. What a title! Comedy of course. You weren't even born. Besides, our Thomas sells paintings, daubings of ships in Gibraltar Bay. Or firing off in the estuary.'

'He says their rooms are cramped.'

'Do you want me to leave *him* this house? Fools. Fishmongers. My wastrel brother. Mother always preferred me; couldn't abide his whining ways. Thomas, his mincing offspring, a starveling, cat-skin, dried neat's tongue, bull's pizzle, stock-fish! Oh for breath to utter.'

'Richard, your age! This cannot do you good.'

'What more? It's all here. I have not forgot a word. Would that I could say it to his face: you tailor's yard, you sheath, you bow case, you vile standing-tuck!'

'You'll fit yourself to death!'

''Tis not due yet, my girl. Go again. Go further. Don't return without them. Or else bring the lawyer. I'll write a new will.'

She shook her hair, banged out again, her peachy skin flushed.

The first one had blushed like that. He's not thought of her in forty years, that strange soft down. Can recall only her roundness of face, the feel of her skin. She left him rich.

He'd cast around, lost without a woman. Not that it was hard. Women throng to a widower. Anna Maria was twenty-two years younger; she needed his standing with Garrick. It was his pinnacle – Drury Lane. Fame aflame in a thousand tapers. Crowds shoving to get in. She envied him his comic ways. To hold the audience between finger and thumb, feed them gestures, jests, antics till they wept with laughter.

But stately, majestic she had to be tragic. He coached, encouraged, married, loved her. And she supped from him, supped, supped until she grew to her own height. The great roles became hers: Desdemona, Cordelia, Imogen, Cleopatra, Lady Macbeth, Gertrude, Isabella, Medea. She could only impress; could not unbend to comedy. Except in bed where, freed from her costume's drama, hair piled high to terrify, Electra became Birmingham lass.

She was loyal: dismissed flatterers, adulterers. She was no Mrs Robinson. Secretly he admired her acting less than did the public. Too much violence in her rage, ice in her disdain, stature in her revenge. She stalked about the stage; worse, tottered, flumped. He knew how she should do it, but she would no longer be taught.

He who'd once longed to play Hamlet, was forever cast as clown. Emaciated miser, padded Falstaff, Pantaloon. Demand grew for her, fell away from him. The grander she became the weaker he, till it was she who commanded, he who obeyed. Her fine voice pealed through their house, an auditorium; she seemed to grow taller. She was the *grande dame* at all times, he her fool.

Widower again, along comes Elizabeth Jones, quite the

opposite, obedient to his old man's whims for which he loves her. Pretty, occasionally petulant, of scant understanding. He'll keep her till his death, which he doesn't intend for a while. There's spirit in him yet, wit of which she comprehends little: only his friends recognise the sources of his speech. Keep her with good pay, flattery, the promised house.

But now he can't have eels for dinner! Old parts caper in and out of his head like demonic clowns goading him with *mots justes*. 'I am provoked into a fermentation, as my Lady Froth says, "Was ever the like read of in Story!"' No eels! His life is a comedy.

The great parts could have been his. He'd had it in him to sit upon the ground like Richard, weep like Othello, howl like Lear. But they've lived in his head, on his shelves, breathed only as longings beneath the comic habit. Anna Maria drank his power. Died of dropsy. All that's left for him is to keep hold of Elizabeth, write his will five times, order dinner.

No *eels*! Can he believe her? Young thing, empty head under those black Welsh locks. Purchased because he couldn't live without a woman. She'll out to the starveling Thomas on the corner, he thinks, who'll perceive her glowing skin with his painter's eye. Her features delightfully tense with temper. His wife expecting their sixth. Irresistible. Where? Where? His blood heats. His eyes start. She'll bring him into the kitchen of course. Cook up eels together. They'll to it. The youthful body she wants. While I sit here. He fights a surge of sleep. His heart tightens, bites. Head beats its blood-knell. They'll to it while I nod. While I snore off-stage, a comic *vieillard*.

She returns later, tired, tetchy, her basket heavy with young eels, silver like those his mother cooked. Finds him still in his chair, his head on his arms on the table, the handwritten manuscript of *M. Soupe-Maigre* within reach. He is dead. In her fright the basket spills its contents round him, an ironic, fishy aura.

She scoops them up and tearful, sends the boy for Dr Cruickshank.

'Mr Yates has had an apoplexy.'

'I heard him rant and rave,' the boy says.

She darts about the room, unsure what to do.

'Poor old man,' she thinks and immediately feels relief. No more running to his call, dodging his grasp, finding excuses to avoid his bed. Fumbling, tumbling.

The house is hers. He's shown her the will. Stafford Row, Pimlico! A fine address. She paces around, pleased, then nervous, as if pieces might each vanish at her look. Turns to see if Richard has woken up.

She'll have soirées, music, dancing. Invite whom she wants. She will be desired.

She thinks of Thomas Yates. He finds her attractive. But he desires the house more. Five, soon six children, weary wife. Richard had always scorned him; mocked her worries. Suddenly she understands that in willing her the house he's willed her Thomas Yates and family. She spins round to remonstrate, gasps, startled at the body. Sobs for a while.

Four months later a gun fires accidentally in the hands of John Sellers, one of two men she's hired to protect her from Yates's persistence. Thomas dies of his wounds. At the Old Bailey, Sellers gets six months and a fine of one shilling for manslaughter. Elizabeth Jones is acquitted of murder.

Richard would surely laugh at this comic turn for the worse. The chaffless Elizabeth will not be able to keep six children and their poor widowed mother from her door.

But that's to come. Now, before Cruickshank arrives, she wipes away the slime from where the fish fell. Eels! She takes them to the kitchen to use for funeral baked meats.

LAPLAND

The occasion was magnificent. A gala to celebrate the King's recovery from madness. Attended by court, nobility, persons of distinction, women dazzling in white and garter blue, the oldest bearing purple trains.

Long tables laid in silver, the royal in gold, lit by forty two-branched candlesticks. Like reindeer antlers, thought Edward Gage, accompanying his father, a baronet close to the King. Two pages supported the old man when he stood. Otherwise, gouty, apoplectic, he sat peering irritably at figures shifting across filmed vision.

Supper was sumptuous, exceeding anything seen before in the kingdom. Twenty tureens of soup preceded all kinds of fowl: ducks, cygnets, green geese, young turkey, rails, chicken; with asparagus, peas, beans. These also came cold, boned, swimming or standing on dishes of jelly supported by paste pillars no thicker than a knitting needle. Crayfish pies, ham and brawn in masquerade, four foot high temples housing stories of sweetmeats, hothouse fruits fresh, dried, in syrup.

The wager surfaced on a swell of frivolity. Once royalty, the old and infirm had retired, dancing and social intercourse began. For Edward a familiar pattern: flirtatious teasing from tipsy women, sparring from men. Women resented his lack of desire for them; his fine bearing, generous income lost to books, collecting, obsession with dull, faraway places. Men resented the women's resentment. Remarks sharpened and flew.

'If snowy wastes are so fascinating, dear Edward, why do you not go and live there?'

'He would languish without his curiosities! He must touch and caress them every day.'

'He prefers his collection to company, I swear it! He ignores us, even in our best attire,' shaking elaborate curls beneath her 'God Save the King' bandeau.

'I'd wager ten thousand pounds he'd prefer your company to some ice-cold, snow-capped Lapp woman!'

Gibing finally provoked. Inebriated, having drunk rather than danced, Edward agreed to the wager's ridiculous terms: return in six months with two Lapp women and two reindeer.

Days later his father died, he inherited the estate, had no need of ten thousand pounds. Yet he prepared carefully, packed cases of wine, spirits, salt, tobacco, jewellery, boarded the *Splendid* and sailed for Christiania and the wild North.

*

Letters home gave Edward's instructions for return in early November, within the agreed time. A large room was made ready for the Lapp women, who, it seemed, were sisters. Furniture was uncovered, fires lit, supplies of meat and fish ordered. Anticipation pulsed among his neighbours.

Edward was a mystery to his peers. His interests were not shared, thought more suitable for old men. At best he was comical, a useful butt, at worst irritatingly abstruse, aloof. Mrs Clavering, celebrated for youthful indiscretions, failed in her ambition to take him in hand.

Adored by his short-lived mother, he'd been a gentle boy, almost effeminate. He wandered the estate through bilberries and gorse-covered forts; collected birds' eggs, paying boys in tied cottages to bring more. Set them out tenderly. In winter months, after a pint of port, his widowed father abandoned attempts to remove him from the library. Oneiric hours filled Edward's mind with other worlds.

The baronet resolved to push his son out on the grand tour. Edward was delighted. Words, architectural plans, engravings became flesh, stone, heat, colour, Nature. He moped among ruins, sketched, scribbled. He learned how much to give for desired objects. Haggled. Took lessons in love from the Roman demi-monde; thereafter only found women desirable who laughed in a foreign tongue.

He bought the usual classical fragments, but travel and inexhaustible funds bit like addiction. He'd take a common thing, seek every variation: Japanese silk shoes, Pyreneean espadrilles, Indian wooden clogs, Moroccan leather slippers; funerary flasks and caskets from crude to exquisite; scores of coffee pots.

He loved natural objects made more extraordinary by human ingenuity: carved hornbill skulls, ivory powder horns, a geometrically perfect nautilus shell painted with the Spanish naval defeat of 1639; snuff boxes, cups, knife handles, rings of jade, cornelian, lapis, amethyst, nephrite; a tiny cameo of reindeer in pink agate. He built an extension to the library with countless cupboards, glass cases, batteries of drawers. Encouraged his servants to look and be amazed; never imagined collectors among them.

Edward's excursion to Lapland had been difficult within the wager's time-limit. It was summer when he arrived in Norway:

lack of bread, wine and salt in the far north mattered little in the exhausting beauty of the light. His gifts swiftly bought the two sisters from their father, such was the value of tobacco and spirits, gold brooches, bangles.

Demonstration of success completed the wager. On the Herefordshire estate with its mountainous backdrop, neighbours and friends saw picturesque reindeer nibbling last leaves beyond the ha-ha; found the Lapp sisters quite acceptable, their features almost delicate, figures shapely, clothed not in mephitic skins but dresses of coarse cloth, with belts, necklaces of silver and copper. The two women stood by timidly as Edward explained his hoard of Lappish artefacts, encouraged his guests to try morsels of dried fish and reindeer meat.

Perhaps there was disappointment at the women's pleasantness, their shy smiling. Two more decorative oddities in Edward's collection. The guests had hoped for signs of disorder, feculence, something more deliciously rancid.

Edward's obsession with Lapland had begun years earlier in his father's library where he'd found John Schefferus's *History of Lapland* on a distant shelf. The book, already antique, promised '*a new World difcovered*' where lives were lived in hunger, cold, solitude. Edward already liked solitude. In the first year of his reading he tried all three, striking out in wintry Marcher dusk, shivering beneath rocks at midnight with half a game pie. His paltry stick fire died, the cold skewered his bones, he stamped and chanted a mesmeric declension:

Immel	*Immele*	*Immela*
Immel	*O Immel*	*Immelist*
Immeleck	*Immeliig*	*Immewoth*
Immeliidh	*O Immaeleck*	*Immaeliie*

By the time of the wager swathes of Schefferus were committed to memory; he knew well what deprivations to expect, what attitudes to anticipate. Anni and Mari were Christian. He could take them to church but they might need more; he purchased certain stones, drums with brass rings, deer's horn hammers for divination.

He'd read of the Lapps' 'immoderate luft'; both sexes, all ages slept in the same hut. Blushing, he accused himself of accepting the wager because of it. Yet the Lapps also esteemed marriage, said the book, rarely violated it.

On the return voyage the sisters stayed below deck and for a week after their arrival wouldn't come out of their room, in which, Edward understood, his housekeeper eventually washed off smoke-grime. When finally they appeared, how charmed he was by their penetrating dark eyes, exotic smallness, broad breasts, slender waists, their childlike pleasure at his glittering gifts! That was how he wanted them, beautiful, innocent; to admire, to learn from.

Of necessity there had been a small exchange of vocabulary, though Edward was not a natural linguist. He was *albma* – a *gentleman*, he told them, Mari was *kiscardasche* – a *sister* of Anni, at which they giggled. He would be *wellje* – like a *brother*, he said, but they looked dismayed, speaking words of which he recognised none. He struggled to explain that they should sleep in beds, not on the ground, convinced them only by gestures. Under shaggy reindeer skins, according to household gossip, they slept naked.

He instructed his cook to lightly boil the reindeer meat kept in the ice-house (*jenga kaote* – ice shed: he was pleased with that). This satisfied Mari and Anni while it lasted; they rejected tasteless mutton, vegetables. Reported pulling at raw topside in one of the pantries, he bribed them with bracelets and smiles, understood their need, sent out a man to catch trout.

One of the reindeer had to be killed. By now it was summer: Mari and Anni placed strips of meat along the terrace balustrade to dry in the sun. Around the plinths of Pan, Bacchus, Mnemosyne and Jupiter in shepherd garb. In late afternoon crows grew bold. Dried meat was abandoned.

They foraged for berries in the kitchen gardens, annoying gardeners, delighting Edward with their pleasure and stained fingers. He explained to Cook how burying a dish of boiled strawberries in the earth was a hedge against winter. He wanted everyone in his household to learn.

Looking from his window on a wonderful July night, he saw Mari and Anni gather leaves below the terrace, lay out reindeer skins on them, lie down to sleep in the full moon. On subsequent nights, they moved to another patch of ground, speeding agilely over the grass with their leaf mattresses and skins.

Following the description in Schefferus, whose illustrations greatly excited the women, Edward helped build a tent, stretching woollen, linen, skins obliquely across poles, ramshackle but dry enough, with a smoke hole at the top. There they'd sit after a day swiftly sweeping the estate for fruit, embroidering winter gloves and caps with stars, flowers, birds, reindeer, knots, spangles of gold and silver thread. And there at the opening they welcomed Edward in, into the smoke-filled warmth.

*

Robert Sanders was small, brawny, unflappable, with practical ingenuity grown out of years of difficult employment by a woman of notoriety. At her death her daughter dismissed him with sorrow. He took another unusual post, helping Edward Gage with his collecting. Edward found Robert an excellent help-meet, common-sensical, unromantic, utterly unlike himself.

Tales of Edward's past poured into Robert's ear when

he arrived, gossip, rumour which, though years old, shone with repeated telling, sparkled with semi-precious phrases.

It seems that Edward had fallen in love with two Lapp women.

For months he'd spoken of nothing else, courted the women with gifts, created a stir taking them about in his vis-à-vis, conducted them one on each arm to church, eaten their dried fish and meat. Was seen on his knees outside their tent chanting from a book in Lappish tongue. A sharp-eyed maid found the translation in his script. One verse, ripped from the rest, was passed from hand to hand of those who could read:

What stronger is than bolts of steel?
What can more surely bind?
Love is stronger far than it,
Upon the Head in triumph she doth sit:
Fetters the mind,
And doth controul,
The thought and soul.

An honourable man, not one to court scandal, what could he do? Hardly marry both of them. Nor, as Christians, would they have agreed to it.

In others' telling, the tale was of lust not love. The naked, black-haired doxies bewitched him with their magic, reading the runes of their drum with its palimpsest of little figures drawn as if by fingers in blood; its jingling rings. They invoked spectres, demons in the wood and drew him in with their repetitive songs until he was no longer master of himself. The sounds that came from that construction of skin and twigs! Such laughter!

Whichever version he heard, the story-tellers agreed on one thing: mushrooms brought all to an end.

Edward's estate contained ancient woods into which as summer died the women moved their tent. Warmth lingered into autumn and gorgeous *amanita muscaria* burst up through the mould. Later, shrivelled stalks and caps were found on a sill in the hottest kitchen, but at first there was no explanation for the climactic event.

One night the women staggered up the stone steps as if drunk and collapsed on the terrace. From attic windows, from behind shutters, eyes stared, mouths gaped as the women's bodies twitched in convulsions then fell into deep sleep. The impatient went to bed. Edward was in his library, didn't know. Suddenly, stupefied but awake the women rose, made frenzied movements. Someone called Edward who now saw the women cavort, stretch their arms in wildness, step with enormous strides over tiny growths of lichen between the flags, crying out.

Soon after, the fly agaric was found, drying, ready to be swallowed. Edward made arrangements once again for travel to Lapland.

His public explanation was the Lapp women's homesickness. He must return them to the land for which they longed. Few believed him. For years stories entertained his neighbours and friends, sustained the servants. Yet most made an effort to hide their mirth when he returned after six months, aged, melancholic, increasingly irritable like his father.

He turned away from the north, travelled south and east. Robert, fair-minded, wise, made no judgment of the tales. He was pleased to travel, arrange, carry, organise Edward's comfort and his own. He picked up languages remarkably well so that even procuring was easy in foreign lands. Edward preferred two women, laughter.

The collection grew, its fame spread. Scholars visited though Edward was often alone with his curiosities. No one saw his nightly inspection of cribs, his gentle stroking of the Lappish carrying cradle like a small boat out of water.

A TULIP SKY

A disorderly parcel was handed in at the Turkish Embassy. It was brought by a boy who, panting, had carried it some distance through dung-thick streets to ever grander gateways. Painstakingly written on the outer covering was: *to xlensee turckush ambassad* with decorative flourishes beneath. Brown paper, too much thin hemp rope, newspaper and household cloths had been used to wrap five handsome copper coffee pots.

There was no indication who'd sent the parcel and the boy fled, intimidated by armed, turbaned guards at the door. The pots gleamed with years of polishing, but the embassy kitchen was fully equipped with similar vessels, so dust soon dulled them in a far pantry.

Alice White had watched the wrapping, waiting to demonstrate her writing skill and earn three pence. She tried unsuccessfully to charge more for the flourishes. She was a canny young woman, severely cut, constantly critical, certain of a higher destiny. Of course Betsy Hoddy knew more of the world, but she was old and could neither read nor write. Alice would never end up like *her*, unmarried, still a housemaid, senior only by dint of age.

Alice didn't know the pots had been stolen. Over several years Betsy had secreted each one into her box of clothing. They'd come from a vast collection of curiosities belonging to a previous employer. The thefts were never discovered, Betsy eventually left and in her final employment she'd felt free to display all five on her meagre mantlepiece. As head housemaid in a newly-built country house she had a room of her own under the eaves, warmed by a tiny coal fire. Here, when not buffing the pink-tinged copper, she contemplated clouds and stars through the roof window, her only light. The younger maids admired the pots, curvaceous, exotic, glowing in the firelight. They accepted her vague explanation, quickly forgot them.

Alice was wrong to make no connection between the parcel and Betsy's new-found piety. She assumed increased church-going was just a feature of old age. Betsy was often in a huddle with the curate. She placed an unopened prayer book on the deal table by her bed and sometimes mumbled as if in prayer. The prayer book had gold-edged pages. Betsy ran her fingers along its closed goldenness and felt doubly blessed.

She had never made a living from thieving, hadn't the wit, but she knew a lovely thing when she saw it. At fourteen she was sacked from employment as a kitchen maid in Red Lion Street. Mrs Nancy Mason found her rifling her drawers, placing silver thimbles on each of her fingers. Mrs Mason had always been exacting but her anger on this occasion was unprecedented.

Betsy returned to her East Anglian village, walking for several days, arriving faint and unwelcome at the shack from which young mud-bound siblings ran out.

'What a come back for?' her mother shouted. 'What will a eat? Got rid of a last time. What a come back for?'

Her father had taken her up to London and left her. It was extraordinary that she had found harmless employment, retained her virtue, for she was comely, her face a soft symmetry, her peasant origins suggested only by slight squareness of jaw and hand. And now she was back, prettier than before, a burden to indigent parents.

At first she refused to sleep in the bed with the rest of the children, but winds from the North Sea drove her to it. She wore her kitchen maid's shoes until they dropped to pieces, combed her hair enough to draw disparaging comment. She proved her value when the father fell into a mill race and drowned, leaving her to gather wood, trap rabbits and, had she wanted to, while away hours smoking on an upturned trough. She was still there at eighteen, knowing she should leave, her resolve impoverished.

*

It is August. Betsy kicks carefully through stubble, taking a longer route to delay her tasks. The edge of the wood is still; birds, leaves, too exhausted to flinch. In the heat only insects thrive. She stops by a mound high as her knees to watch wood ants running back and forth, carrying twigs as big as their bodies, eggs, carcases.

Men's voices, nearing. She backs behind a great pine in time to see two figures hurrying along the dirt road she's just left. Glimpses moustaches, long and black, extraordinary clothes, colours. They carry a heavy wheel between them, presumably taking it to the wheelwright; a carriage broken down.

Alert now, she hears more voices and follows the sound, but parallel to it, into the wood. Here is the clearing, bright with fractured light, where she sometimes sits and dreams. She makes for a thicket of ash sprouts and elder to watch.

She's never seen men like this before. They wear huge turbans of white and red, long-sleeved jackets, voluminous striped trousers, flat boots, belts with daggers. Several unroll an immense carpet, drive brass poles into the ground, raise a canopy over it. Others cast around for wood – Betsy shrinks into her thicket – drag logs together and light a fire.

The leader appears. A man both tall and round, bearded, turbaned, dressed in a long green silk coat patterned with leaves and sinuous stalks, he sits cross-legged on the carpet, made comfortable with cushions. From a tripod over the fire they hang a pan, measure spoonfuls from a box painted with tulips, pour hot liquid into a small copper vessel, fat-bellied, squat, its beak-spout like a bird Betsy once saw in a print shop window.

Coffee, dark, biting. She knows the smell, if not the taste, from coffee-houses she's passed in the city. Her nostrils and palate are dry; she longs to drink. Excitement and the sound of pouring press on her bladder. She lifts her skirts, plants a leg sideways in a half-crouch, pees on dry leaves and the next minute is hauled out of the thicket by two turbaned men. They carry her off, arguing in their rapid gibberish. She'll always remember how she felt no fear, for all the daggers and the strangeness.

They take her a little way off to where, on another carpet under another canopy's nacreous shade, several women recline on cushions and drink coffee while children sit with them and eat small cakes.

It seems that she stands for minutes, speechless, pressing into the marvellous carpet with her toes, breathing intoxicating coffee fumes as the women question her in their language.

'Don't understand,' she says.

'Turkish,' says one woman, pointing to herself and the others. 'Am-bassa-dor,' she enunciates slowly, pointing away in the general direction of the men.

'Oh, oh. Miss Hoddy,' Betsy says and curtsies.

Some of the younger women pull at Betsy's sleeves and sit her down, bring a bowl and jug. Wash her face, hands and feet in water smelling of roses. Children in silk clothes, like miniature adults, black-eyed, amused, come up and touch her fair hair, stroke it.

For an hour she sits with them under the canopy's tulip sky. They chatter unceasingly without Betsy understanding a word. They bring her a tiny cup in thin china, her rough fingers honoured by its touch; pour coffee into it from another beaked pot with a curving handle, its brass lid shining wheat-gold, like an elegant hat. She sips the sweetest blackness and it seeps into her veins, possesses her body. Her cheeks flush with heat and pleasure. Her eyes are dazzled by smiling plumpness on all sides, half concealed by gauzy kerchiefs, garments of pale pink silk, green, embroidered white, silver thread flowering on gold brocade, glittering bodkins, girdles embedded with lustrous jewels. Her mind fills to its very edges with coruscation to last a life.

WHAT WAS LEFT TO KNOW

From London he took stages to Colchester and Ipswich then walked. He knew the general direction and besides, he wanted to sniff his way to the sea. There was pay in his midshipman's pocket for inns and beef and once they'd wheedled out of him where last he'd sailed and in whose fleet, he went to bed drunker than he'd intended.

Long before he saw the coast he smelled brine in the wind. It was there in the woods, even as his boots scuffed dried puffball husks, rotten stumps of stinkhorns, sank into a thick mire of leaves: all that was left of a rich autumn. Salt stench drew him to the marsh edge, the trodden path, the reeds that once hid everything from him. Soon enough the church tower appeared above the trees.

It was five years since he left, a boy. Now one-and-twenty, he'd seen war and death at sea, loyalty, hatred, victory, injustice. Had been lifted high by the spirit of radicalism, read Tom Paine; heard all about America, the promised land. What was there left to know? No parents would welcome him home, no siblings. Only one person would remember John Airey. He was returning for Margaret.

Dusk and smoke of fires. Remembered shapes: yew tree, wall, shed leaning seawards. He went straight to the house. He knew his adoptive father was dead and had no doubt he'd left the house to Margaret, his housekeeper and erstwhile mistress.

The bell was answered by a young girl who, seeming not to understand, showed him into the parlour. Here, toasting himself before the fire, the new surgeon-apothecary took him for a patient.

No, John explained, he was a visitor hoping to find Margaret Hickling.

'Ah! She it was who sold me the house,' said the surgeon, a ruddy-skinned man of impregnable health. He understood that before her it had belonged to the previous surgeon and pleasant indeed he found it. A little dark perhaps, but situated close to the highway, well-placed for night calls.

John asked if Margaret had moved nearby.

No, he said, she was not in the neighbourhood. She hadn't told him where she was going, though subsequently someone heard she'd gone north. It seems the house had been left her by her widowed employer but she no longer had reason to live in the district.

'The young lad went to sea,' she'd apparently remarked. He studied John's face.

'And did you know her well, Mr . . . ?'

But John wouldn't give his name, thanked the surgeon, glanced round and left. The house was entirely different. Its gloomy rooms, once saturated with the sorrow of his adoptive parents, smiled brightly like their new owner. He spent the night on an alehouse settle well wrapped against spring frost.

He woke early – the settle was hard; he'd rather have

slept in a hammock – and set off northwards.

Those had been the first decisions he'd ever made. To leave the navy. Then *not* to go to America with his friend William Leopard to start a new life, but return instead to the woman with whom he'd enjoyed six carefree months in his youth. Six months of affection, of manhood. Before their discovery. Before his adoptive father's dismay at this betrayal, at the hurtful triumph of youth over age, at John's poor return for years of dull but worthy upbringing. He'd agreed to go away to sea.

Neither Margaret nor he made any promises – she was, after all, his adoptive father's servant and mistress, not his – and they didn't correspond. It had never occurred to him that she wouldn't be there in the house in which he'd spent most of his childhood, waiting for him, ready to resume their joy. Up in the roof of the house where she had her bedroom and he his. Where through the skylight you could hear the sea shift. Wake together to watch clouds scud. For *that* was what was left to know – the comfort of love.

He couldn't think of turning back now. To continue walking was to enter unknown land, an uncertain life. But to return was to re-enter known territory that his mind had left. He had to go on.

For days he walked, spurning no offers of rides in carts and wagons. This was seamen's country: the inhabitants had only to note his midshipman's stripe, hear the name *Ardent* to know his worth. They thought he was off to join his ship in Yarmouth and once there he did indeed wander along the dockside, alert to its signs and moods, yet detached, distracted. Soon he turned into the town where he sauntered vaguely along the smarter streets, hung about the market, glanced down alleys, into doorways at night. Yarmouth was north. But there was a lot more north between there and the Wash.

Back at the quays he watched the loading of ships for battle:

hundreds of wooden boxes of ordnance, ammunition, stores. The town was full of marines. Here it was, laid out for him, recognisable, the world he knew. Arduous, companionable. They would welcome him back. Young, strong, promoted twice in three years, they needed him.

He kept close to the curve of the coast wherever he could. Dipped down to the beach to stare at the waves, as if she might rise out of them. His money ran low but his story kept him fed. And on occasion woken in the night by women younger than Margaret had been back then; for she was older than he by a number of years and already saddened, even though he'd made her smile.

The country changed, woods became rare, fields opened themselves to the sky. Where he could he walked along the beach, his boots cracking wrack and razorshells. On one side flint-grey ocean, on the other mud cliffs scraped by wind and flood, shaped like waves before they break, their crests a spume of grass. Here, in this land, sea ruled. You accepted it, lived off what it gave, grieved for what it took, fishing smacks, men o'war. Villages.

On a blustery day he heard bells ring, tolling without cease. Faint, distant, some village on the way to Cromer; he wouldn't reach the place till late. He hastened but it was quite dark when he arrived, flares had been extinguished, rescue was over for the day. A 74-gun, they said, *The Tremendous*, set sail from Yarmouth, the light good, mid-afternoon, known pilots in charge but a strong tide flowing. More than 500 men on board. Broke up in no time and only two smacks out fishing to haul in the living from the swell. Hit Hammond's Knoll, the worst of the sandbanks. So many ships lost there. So many good men gone. Yes, tomorrow they'd be glad of any help with the sea's harvest.

He joined the line of carts to retrieve those cast up by the morning's high tide, to lay them on boards hastily swept of dung, trundle them back to crowd the churchyard.

The whole village was at the beach sifting through treasures arranged by the artless sea on beds of wrecked shells. Women and children loaded their handcarts with food, linen, casks, little spoiled, so freshly drowned. Men heaved wooden boxes onto wagons, furniture, spars, planks, winters' worth of fuel. It was as if a fair were taking place in the midst of war. People must step over bodies to reach their booty.

John had seen men killed in battle, men with whom he'd eaten, laughed and argued hours before. These were not his companions, yet they were the same: the worn, the untried, hardened, soft-faced. Brave, terrified. Which of them had cried out and to whom had they called? Which had looked inward and found a sudden consolation? Or none. All day the sound of surf and wind pounded in his ears. All day he heard the voice of every man and boy whose body he gently carried to the cart.

'Will you stay?' they asked him in the village. 'We need more seamen.' Later in the week there would be a funeral at a great single grave dug in the glebe next to the church.

No, he told them, when all this is done he'd attend the burial but then he must travel north. He had made up his mind.

'Leave that one,' someone said to him as he bent to lift another corpse the following day. 'He's a local man. Fisherman. Boat capsized when the big one went down. They'll come for him.'

He laid the body on the sand. The weathered face beaten, the huge hands like nets drying.

Margaret came to collect her husband.

Spy

When should a wife spy on her husband?

In Exchange Alley lecherous sparrows fought in the gutters at Battle's. She'd lived there all her life, her father's coffee house. A child playing with the puppy among men's feet, petted by pipe-smokers, removed when the mood became rowdy. Was more familiar with the smell of coffee than porridge. Then for years the comely girl pouring port, claret, porter. Her face drew the men (there were no female customers), caused them to linger, chalk up another. His wife dead, Sam Battle depended on his daughter: she must keep an eye on the poaching, roasting, toasting as well as on him. Waiters in striped waistcoats ran about with coffee, dishes, debt books, but from mid-morning on she must stand behind the curved bar, a reluctant beacon.

Heat and steam from boiling coffee drove her naturally high colour to a perpetual blush. Her strong bare arms prickled. She'd grown to hate compliments; took scant notice of customers. Enjoyed only the exercise of efficiency.

She was no longer Sarah Battle. Had married James Wintrige, clerk in the customs office. He was to be her revolution. Through him she would touch a world of intellect, ideas. He read books, wrote plays, hobnobbed with thinkers. Was always scribbling: when not his own work then letters, minutes for meetings of the London Corresponding Society (those earnest artisans who longed for equality without bloodshed, debated into the night, moved from inn to inn when threatened.) Through him she could surely abandon the tedium of flattery, the stink of tobacco and charred meat that hung about her like a garment, the pain of swollen feet. Learn about, enter a higher sphere.

He'd wooed her with names, knowledge, superiority. A head above the others, she'd seen him watch her, his long fingers resting contemplatively by his frog-thin lips. He dealt her a hand of luminous phrases: Age of Reason; Tree of Liberty; Enlighten the Nation. How could she resist?

They rented rooms in Ossulston Street. He set out his books, his writing table. Gave her pamphlets to read while he wrote. She asked about his meetings, what they discussed, what resolved by democratic vote. He couldn't tell her much. Had to be cautious even with his own wife. She was startled at his severity; stopped asking. Opened a window to catch the early robin song in February.

He said she reminded him of his mother and grandmother who'd brought him up. Their rosy colouring. Forgiving nature. She wondered what he meant. Nightly she carried back food for supper wrapped in several cloths to keep it hot. Flasks of wine. They ate well. Never quarrelled.

Yet five years had barely changed her life. Still she supervised the grinding of beans, measuring of river water in which to boil them; mixing of egg, sugar, milk with chocolate grounds; roasting of venison, stewing of turtle; supply of glasses, clean cloths, coffee dishes.

Chased the dog out of the kitchen. And stood not smiling, ever redder, an accidental siren.

Exhausted at night, she returned to find James writing or out at a meeting till two a.m. His income was erratic. Once he gave up the customs office to pursue the performance of a play he'd written. Went to Margate. A satire on gaming, it closed after one act to howls of derision. She found him head in hands, shaking.

'What is it?'

'No matter,' dry-eyed, resistant.

No, she could not leave the coffee house. They couldn't live without Battle money.

*

James stops going to Battle's to drink. Life for radicals is becoming more difficult. As their numbers increase, government screws tighten. Last year someone was arrested in the coffee house for giving out handbills urging on rioters. This year immense crowds take their families to St George's Fields. Listen to stirring speeches, behave with decorum. Sarah goes, her father's permission drawn like a pulsing tooth.

The June day shines. Sand martins swoop in and out of dirty pools. The great ground is walled between the Obelisk and King's Head prison, surrounded by nervous military. James is there somewhere, making notes to transcribe late tonight. She shows her ticket, seeks a group, the space too huge else. Sits among dock and burdock with wives and children of bakers, shoemakers, cordwainers, a watch-face painter and is swept quite out of herself till she weeps and shouts with the rest, glorying in The Voice of Reason, like the Roaring of the Nemean Lion, issuing even from the Cavern's Mouth! Universal Suffrage! Annual Parliaments! Truth shall be Eternal!

Thousands of elated citizens. But peaceable. No violence. Horse and foot guards slink away unused.

She is inspired. Carries home the day compact in mind and body, kept alive for ever in layers of memory. He's writing up his notes when she arrives home. Puts a long finger to his lips pursed with determination.

At other times bread riots; anti-crimping riots against press-gang cruelty; someone throws a stone at the King's coach. Habeas Corpus is suspended; new acts against seditious activities and treasonable practices drawn up.

A man asks after James one evening. She knows spies sit in every coffee house and inn. He'd warned her to be careful what she said, but she isn't garrulous. Does she know where James Wintrige had been that afternoon?

'I have been here since six o'clock this morning.' She'd heard a thrush sing from a roof ridge on the way. 'He was surely at the customs office today.'

'He was expected at a meeting. Never came.'

She pays no attention; is determined to close by nine. Staying open late causes suspicion nowadays.

Two weeks later he comes again. She wouldn't recognise him if he hadn't spoken, for he's undistinguished in the press of men.

'Thomas Cranch, Mrs Wintrige. Enquiring about your husband again. I'm from the Society.'

'Yes?'

'He is ill, I hear. He sent us a letter today. He's too ill to attend the meeting. Coughing blood.'

Leaning towards him to hear, their foreheads touch. She draws back hastily, sees amusement, pleasure hop across his face. He drinks porter in rapid sips. He is a little man, stout, dark hair cropped, movements energetic. A bookseller and printer.

'Strand. Number 444. Opposite Buckingham Street.'

Or so he says. She warms to him despite herself.

James gets into bed about midnight, undershirt smelling of anxiety.

Half-asleep she asks: 'Are you unwell?'

'No. Been at a meeting.'

'Have you coughed up blood?'

'No. Why do you ask?'

She turns over. Shifts away. He has another woman she realises with indignation. Falls asleep.

She's in Battle's at six, her father grumbling, a waiter late. Fires are laid and lit under the coffee cauldron; in the fireplace where men toast their backsides, pat the dog, read aloud from the newspaper. Floors swept, meat prepared, onions fried.

Another woman. The phrase embeds. Before their marriage there'd been a common law wife. He'd left her. She finds relief in pattern.

Later she remembers a conversation. She knew the men. Radicals, drank at the Red Lion, dropped into Battle's once a month to test the mood.

'Wintrige,' she'd overheard.

'Our old friend Wintrige,' the man called Baldwyn said and laughed. They all laughed: Pyke, Hadfield with the scars over his eye, down his cheek, Harley, the young one. Slapped their thighs.

'Is he honest?' asked Coke.

'Yes, if you can trust a man that foolish, that silly.' They laughed again. Left when the spy Nodder appeared.

It wasn't the Wintrige she knew. The day takes over; she can puzzle no more about it.

He's out when she returns. Dripping wax on his papers she rummages. Books of minutes. Once he'd been president. Endless names, dates, sums, meeting places. Precise reports: harrassed by Blackheath Hundreds; justices terrified the landlord, moved to Angel, High Street; adjourned at three o'clock in the morning; appoint as delegates Jas. Wintrige, Joseph Young. Hydra of Despotism, Strong Arm of Aristocracy, yours with Civic Affection.

Sealed letter addressed to R. Ford. Which has gone the next day.

That night in Ossulston Street they coincide, unusually.

'Who is R. Ford?'

'Ho, ho! Been spying on me, have you?'

'I saw a letter, yes. Is it a man or a woman?'

'A woman? Why should you think that? You, with your apple cheeks!' He pinches them with both hands. 'It's for the Society. Our new strategy. We shall demand a meeting with the Duke of Portland. Don't trouble yourself with thinking. You couldn't understand.'

It's not the sliding eyes that shock but the loud laughter, mirthless.

She has found out nothing about the other woman. Yet their marriage is also nothing. Rare meetings. Pared-down questions; opaque answers from the edge of the mattress.

Winter sets hard. Yesterday's horse-dung frosted. House martins, swifts long flown the city. Carrion crows stalk the streets.

Tom Cranch comes often. Stands sipping and smiling, waiting to hear treasonous tones, she assumes. Yet men are cautious now; he can't have much to report. His own speech is like his drinking, rapid, gratified. She listens. He tells her about America or describes a future where property is unimportant, where everyone votes and no one starves. She reminds herself that he is trying to trap her.

She looks forward to his smile of pleasure, his latest tale of a reformed world. He charms her into speaking, holding his head at an angle, bright-eyed, like a blackbird listening for a worm. He brings her a poem he's written. About Levellers and frugal meals and simple cotts by rippling streams.

She tells him she was in the great crowd at St George's Fields in June among the dandelions and flattened grass. He was there, too. Printed the tickets for it, he says. There've been two huge meetings since. He printed reports of those. Now a final one, near the Jew's Harp House, Marylebone, where city succumbs to open country. The great men will attend, the heroes, to speak against the Acts. Will she come?

A sudden surge of men from the street breaks her imagined flight.

'Three bottles of your best claret to begin!' they order, roaring.

'What a man you are, Byng! Bagged woodcock near St Martin's and snipe at Five Fields. Will you cook them, Miss Battle, when they've hung enough?'

'Yes,' she says to the men who never noticed her marriage. 'No,' replies in a low voice to Cranch when they've moved away.

She doesn't think her father will let her go, she says. It was bad enough last time. Bawled red in the face about the mob. His gout is like the fiend.

Some nights James doesn't come home at all. She needs evidence if she is to accuse him. To avoid a lofty denial, cold laugh. She rummages again, more extensively. This time, something. Is under the table picking up torn foolscap when the door rattles.

He doesn't come in; it rattles more. Furtive knocking. She gathers the shreds together and into a pocket; opens a crack.

'Please let me in,' says Tom Cranch. 'I've escaped from the spunging house. Bailiffs won't think to come here.'

She draws the bolt behind him.

'Ran through my money.' He's breathing heavily. 'Reports of general meetings all printed by me – T. Cranch, Printer at the Tree of Liberty, no. 444 Strand, opposite Buckingham

Street – and no payment! Bailiffs broke in, took me up. The man was drunk. There was a window.'

His eyes are wild with urgency. She could stroke his dark cropped head.

'I must leave the country. Besides, the Acts will be passed at the end of the month. There's nothing for it. Boat to Philadelphia. Come with me.'

He needs her money. Embraces her with undeniable energy. Relish.

She stuffs a bag with clothes, a loaf, her store of cash. He watches her cast the shreds of foolscap from her pocket all over Wintrige's papers, snatch up an undelivered letter.

Screeching gulls left behind. When sea-sickness has passed they huddle together, fend off icy blasts. Rip open the undelivered letter to R. Ford.

> *During the whole of the last five years I am sure, sir, I was always regular in my reports to you and anxious to do everything in my power for the service of government. Not a person on earth, not even my own wife knew of my connection at your office. You know yourself had I been discovered it would have been attended with much personal danger. My part was ever to declaim their beliefs and my disguise to cover myself by folly and silliness.*

Spy. Spy to spymaster. No other woman.

Half-way to Philadelphia. They eat the bread, swear to be true.

LASCIA CH'IO PIANGA

BREAD WILL BE
SIXPENCE THE QUARTERN
if the people will assemble at the
Cornmarket on Monday.

Fellow Countrymen!
How long will ye quietly and cowardly suffer
yourselves to be thus imposed upon and
half starved by a set of mercenary slaves and
government hirelings? Can you still suffer
them to proceed in their extensive monopolies
while your families are crying for bread? No!
Let them exist not a day longer; we are the
sovereignty; rise then from your lethargy. Be at
the Cornmarket on Monday.

*

With downpayments and annuity Mrs Clavering bought a sizeable house in Jermyn Street. Contingent upon return of Lord F's letters. She furnished it with taste: exotic hangings, old masters, new, patriotic seascapes (*A Two-Decker Firing a Morning Gun in the Thames Estuary*), highest quality mattresses. Found girls with good looks, respectable backgrounds. Schooled them in posture and conversation; employed singing, keyboard, dancing masters. Paid out pounds for silks at Kings's, trimmings at Price's in Tavistock Street. On every floor, bookcases sat in corners of delicately painted rooms; moss roses and carnations scented the air; spinets waited.

No flying leap for half a crown *here* or a night's lodging for five shillings and a bottle of wine. Let alone she who'd satisfy your wishes in Green Park for three pence and a dram. The price was five guineas, fifty for a virgin. And such was the quality of Mrs Clavering's that some men were content to play cards, converse, listen to exquisite Harriet Sayles sing Haydn airs.

Attention to detail, above all discretion and order enabled visitors to feel entirely at home or, in the case of the slightly inferior, positively elevated. Mrs Clavering's own wit and good looks, though sharpened with age, enhanced the delight of all who came. Her background was impeccable; she had some French, a little Italian. Enough of everything to attract the noblest from nearby St James's.

Joseph Young, who'd fixed the bill to the Monument without being seen was absorbing Milton when he wasn't reading Tom Paine. His mind oscillated between Latinate syntax and common man's rhetoric, even as his burin dug into metal plate. Apprenticed to an engraver, his days were filled with images. But it was word-cut images that leapt within him. The sketchbook in his pocket contained as many phrases as drawings. Despite natural gentleness he longed for just conflict. At secret meetings friends sought his stirring phrases; notices were written in his well-taught hand. He was growing a pamphlet, a tender, wayward sprout in his brain's packed soil.

When the crowds gathered he stood on the margin, knowing how it would go. Hissing, hustling, pelting with mud. Mealmen, cornfactors, Quakers the target. He didn't shift with the tide as it grew, dispersed, reformed. He wished for sudden unavoidable immersion, but stood, pressed against a wall, tall, thin, black hair tied back, peering, myopic. Mud became brickbats, stones. He heard the riot act, turned away west. Not desertion; self-preservation. A strong sensation of mental power welled in him. He would be ready soon. Even before the apprenticeship was complete at the end of the year. Ready to address his fellow men, to move, compel. How long will your families cry for bread?

The education of Mrs Clavering's girls was not confined to Jermyn Street. She took the most beautiful to superior masquerades to mix with the best names in town; a guinea subscription for each was well worth it. For a select few there were outings to the theatre. Mrs Clavering was fond of the theatre. Even more the opera. When offered the use of his silver ticket by Mr Simpson she took it with delight.

So to the King's Theatre, Haymarket, in expensive, not quite ostentatious gown and headdress. But she experienced only the delicious smell of candles, hair grease, powder, pomade, sweated velvet, dust of the stage: the delicious smell of anticipation. She was turned away by the proprietor.

Mr Simpson took proprietor Taylor to law. His ticket was paid for, he'd lent it in good faith to an old friend, all was legitimate. Mrs Clavering, in sober dress, was called before chief justice Sir J. Easton. Was declared by Taylor's lawyer, obviously and notoriously an exceptionable character, improper to be admitted to the pit of the King's Theatre. Cross-examined, she admitted she'd kept a large house in Jermyn Street for twenty years, was in the habit of letting out the same to ladies who were generally esteemed handsome and sometimes to single gentlemen. His lordship leaned towards her kindly, as so he should, said she was not bound to incriminate herself further. Yet he found against Simpson. Taylor could object to whom he wanted, especially for seats in the pit where persons of the highest rank and fashion usually assembled.

Mrs Clavering was incensed by the hypocrisy. Easton was keeping his nose clean (what was left of it, she told herself, coarsely.) While she lost no money over the case – visits increased through commiseration, especially those of the chief justice – it was most disagreeable to feature in the print shops for so many weeks.

Order and discretion. Necessary for all strands of life. The chaos of France lurched dangerously close. Constant sea victories were needed to show where right lay, for revolution at home could not be countenanced. The poor must be fed into quiescence even if that meant substituting herring for bread, someone suggested, three per person daily, two a penny salted. The rich could abstain from pastry.

Joseph strode down Fleet Street, through Temple Bar, past Strand whores, Charing Cross carriages, wagons, the stocks empty now, but not for long. He felt pulled towards the places of power to where, had this been Paris, the multitude would have surged. *We are the sovereignty now!* His great vision – addressing a vast crowd in St George's Fields – shone before him. *Rise then from your lethargy!* Lethargy was real enough, induced through inanition. Days-old mouldy bread or none at all. Not that he longed for blood: the horrors of France disgusted him, but haunted him too, so near were they to the principles in which he believed – liberty, reform, humanity. Here, as he neared St James's, lived ministerial hirelings, court jugglers, corrupt, licentious, vice-riddled, *a band of parasites living in luxurious indolence out of the public taxes*. If only he could write like Paine!

Up Haymarket where triumphant crows cawed on rooftops, dodging militia in Pall Mall, he slipped in fresh dung, knocked himself out on the shaft of a passing carriage. Returning with boxes, packages, Mrs Clavering stepped down gingerly, irritated at the inconvenience, had him carried insensible into the back of her house.

He ran a fever, was delirious. Was convinced a nest of despots lived at the dark end of the corridor where he lay. That it grew,

> *Thick swarmed both on the ground and in the air,*
> *Brusht with the hiss of rustling wings.*

He almost gave himself away. Books were found when his stinking clothes were removed, exchanged; a sketchbook of indecipherable doodles and writing; yet it was concluded that his brow and thigh were noble and besides he was too far west to have been involved in the Cornmarket riot.

He came round to the smell of delectable ragout. Veal, most like. He was wrapped in a blanket on a bench, evidently outside a kitchen. A maidservant stared into his face.

'Where am I?'

'They call it a nunnery,' she said. Ran off, stifling giggles.

He knew at once. Had helped engrave the anonymous series: *The Lady Abbess leaves her celebrated nunnery. The Lady Abbess arrives with due pomp at the K---'s Theatre. The Lady Abbess is trounced by a tailor…*

He must get out. It was the last place he should be – awash with court corruption! There were phrases to write down, phrases that strode with him when he fled the Cornmarket. He sat up, swung his legs round and fell at the blast of pain in his ankle. On his knees he struggled to push himself up just as Mrs Clavering appeared.

'You cannot walk unaided. I'll have Kelly and Page carry you upstairs.'

There, with little grace, the footmen dropped him onto an elegant sofa. Still dazed – someone had administered laudanum – he perceived a dazzle of textures, gleaming objects. Reached for his spectacles, but the coat was not his. Two young women stood to one side, impertinent breasts jutting above Grecian folds. He smelled their scent, the chocolate they sipped.

'Leave us, girls. I would speak with Mr Young.'

Even without eyeglasses he saw the wonderful accuracy of his master's draughtmanship. Mrs Clavering's authority was not confined to her dress. Her bearing was queenly, her nose emphatic. The rouge he'd hand-painted not a disguise for sunken cheeks; her profile fine, magisterial. No wonder Taylor had objected. She'd not look out of place in the royal box.

'I am sorry for your injuries, Mr Young. You were careless.'

'I …' A goldfinch sang sweetly in a brass cage.

'You have been well tended, however. Your clothes have been changed, a surgeon has bound your ankle, relieved your pain; you have been nourished.'

It would make a good tale for the newspapers, the rescue of the young man from his unfortunate accident – her girls real nuns of mercy. Then, for she had no doubt of his sympathies, she would play the good citizen, exposing the revolutionary, traitor to his country. Taylor could hardly turn her away from the King's Theatre after that.

'I am grateful to you, Madam. Please allow me to leave.'

'Wait. I have the contents of your pockets. And you will need help to return home. It's surely too far to stumble on crutches.'

He looked away. She knew. At any moment, she would deliver him up to some pox-ridden fop, some vicious, powdered … some *grand infernal Peer*. He heard music above. The sound of running footsteps, a man's shout, laughter.

She watched him. He was rightly named, she thought, young. His demeanour so serious that she longed to break it, make him laugh. He reminded her of Edward Gage years ago: the more he'd resisted the harder she'd tried.

'I don't much fancy this one,' she said, handling the

thumbed volume. '*Paradise Lost*. What pleasure can there be in that?' She gave it to him.

'*The mind and spirit remains invincible!*' he declaimed, snatching it from her.

Had she been younger she'd have sat herself next to him, close, made him sweat. Made him nestle the goldfinch between her breasts. Nowadays she received attention only from old men. Like Sir J. Easton, whose tastes required her two most hardened girls. Whose pockets were no doubt stuffed with Keyser's Pills even while he'd wielded his power over her in the court, playing kindly one moment, condemning her to public sneers the next. Too long concealed, revulsion against the old rake spread its heat through her body.

'And this, Mr Young. *The Rights of Man*. Is this not a banned book?'

'It is a book that tells the truth, that stirs the mind and heart. That everyone should read in this benighted world. A very jewel of a book.'

'By heavens, then I'll keep it if I may.'

He blinked. 'If you will read it. Read it and learn.'

She suppressed a guffaw. Observed his taut calves as he struggled once more to rise. Could she keep him here longer? She was damned if she'd surrender him to anyone. Let the chief justice enjoy his whipping under the same roof as a revolutionary! Let Taylor stew!

'Wait. I should compensate you in some way for my errant coachman, Mr Young.'

'Please let me go. I must return to my work.'

'Stirring up the minds of the populace, no doubt.'

He groaned with impatience, impotence. Lord! She had forgotten the charms of the incorruptible. He'd certainly never had a woman. And the house was full of girls who were more adept than she'd ever been.

She drank his vulnerable defiance, strong yet sweet like

chocolate. In the next room, chords announced Harriet's voice. A Handel aria. Listening, she saw him listen, flinch at music of thrilling sorrow. *Lascia ch'io pianga*. On and on. No. She wouldn't give him to one of the girls; not even her best.

Deposited by the coachman at his master's above the bookseller and printshop in Aylesbury Street, Joseph was welcomed back by a man who disliked his opinions, admired his skill. A broken ankle was no hindrance to a good engraver. A witty rendering of the Cornmarket riots awaited him, the mob ragged and vicious, led by unshaven ruffians in French revolutionary dress, setting fire to bread shops.

When his apprenticeship was over he'd choose what subjects to engrave. Etch his own designs not those of others. Until then he must take on this task, cut cleanly into the metal plate. Live in his mind: rehearse grand phrases of his pamphlet, recite lines of Milton, paragraphs of Paine, whatever he could to quell the melody that threatened to out-sing them all.

MAD

I, Robert Sanders, with five years' schooling, was help-meet to Edward Gage. I accompanied him to southern Europe, Ottoman and Attic lands, India; collecting vessels, ritual objects, tiny carvings, stones, statues, shards; beautiful, strange. I learned how much straw, sacking, how many planks were required to box and transport what Edward bought. Dealt with removers, stowers, reliable carriers; learned about pack-horses and shipping routes. Evolved a method of communication in every language, though I spoke none. My brain grew balloon-like with knowledge. I developed a love for decorative knife-handles.

I'm a small man, not much to look at, but strong. There's nothing I cannot lift. For years people turned to me: my calm, certainty, they said. I've grown to believe it of myself. I surmount all difficulties. I'm never fazed. Edward was entirely dependent upon me.

We were constantly abroad. When home, he was morose, refused all social engagements. Sent me to conduct visiting scholars around the collection, dispense with them as soon as possible. He would catalogue and place the pieces we'd brought back, create new groupings, rearrange old categories; speak to no one but me. Wouldn't move from the library. He said he'd spent long periods there as a boy, dreaming; as a man he spent much longer periods, the regular domestic round dissolving under his detached stare. He slept, if he slept, on a couch in the extension he'd built to house the collection. He washed rarely, changed his linen less often, ate when I could persuade him.

I'd never travelled north with him. When I first arrived, I was sceptical of the tales about him and the Lappish women. I'm not impertinent; I wouldn't question him. Pieced together for myself all I needed to know.

He was ravished by Lapland. When young he'd read everything known, steeped himself in Schefferus's *History* of the place. Then, because of a stupid wager, he'd travelled there, come back with two reindeer and two Lappish women. Had learned more. The women went back. I could see he was haunted; understood from gentle intimations there was a child.

He sought to expel desolation through travel south, east, incessant buying. The collection became huge. Yet each return to his neglected estate reawoke the discord. Rejected in Lapland, he recreated it in Herefordshire. Knew it wasn't the place itself (that summer light could never come again, he said), but fusing knowledge, memories, precious objects, believed it was.

Come winter solstice he moved his couch to the north end of the collection room, its window tree-darkened, cases and drawers full of Lappish artefacts. Each day he read a portion of Schefferus, chanted repetitively. Made fires from a great pile of sticks, encouraging smoke into the room, begriming his face and hands. Sat for long hours unmoving in a space apparently cramped by shadowy bodies.

In summer he slept outside. Became lively. I helped rebuild the Lapp women's tent, its poles and material an infested heap at the back of a stable. He had clothes made from reindeer skins, the women's bedding. Ate fish mashed with boiled strawberries, dried meat shredded with a whalebone knife. Blood boiled in water to the consistency of hasty pudding. He persuaded known poachers to hunt game with him on his own land. The same men he'd paid for birds' eggs when they'd all been boys.

I knew that neighbours and servants were greatly entertained. Edward had always been unfathomable, people said. They listened eagerly for tales to enliven winter months.

It was poachers who told of prostration before trees, of rock 'altars'. The runes drum with its jingling rings. Then everyone saw him daub the church doors with stick-like men and beasts and ran to restrain him. He was a tall man, fought them, struck out windmill arms, injured someone.

I'd seen the magistrate gawp and laugh behind his hand at other times. But his estate bordered Edward's. He felt embarrassment of class, dismissed the crime as lunacy, ordered confinement.

Opinions ran about like rats: madness was curable, a distemper of the body, like gout or asthma; it was caused by weather, such extremes of heat and cold these days; by too much rich food; too much inactivity in the library; too much travel in foreign lands.

'Let him take Balm of Gilead daily,' someone instructed me. 'I could not live without it,' he said in an exhalation of brandy, cardamom, Spanish fly. The servants were sure it was the Lappish women who'd addled his mind and body with their heathen ways. The things they'd seen and heard!

Edward had no family. The end of his line. Neighbours, worried by threat of anarchy, named a private asylum in

London. I begged to keep him at home. Was ignored. Edward consented to what he thought was punishment.

The owner was Dr Foart.

'Nowadays we use *management* for the insane,' he told me when I left Edward, exhausted, asleep.

'What prison is this?' Edward had said, seeing comfortable, almost elegant furniture, a window without bars.

'Neither beating, mechanical restraints, purges of white and black hellebore, nor spring blood-letting. Management not medicine. And *analysis*.' He tapped a newly-bound volume on the table in his fine study. His house for the reception of insane persons was advertised 'in an excellent air, near the City, for persons of condition only'. Was once a manor house on the corner of Ashby Street. Painted, papered, superior.

Foart was modern. Quick-witted, scholarly. Prurient, bullying. I read the title: Alexander Crichton's *Inquiry into the Nature and Origin of Mental Derangement*.

'I have attended his lectures at the Westminster Hospital, Mr Sanders.'

'I know nothing of mad-doctors,' I said.

'I need as many details of Edward Gage's life as you can give me for my analysis.'

'Ask him yourself, sir.'

'You have been close to him. You have observed him intimately. What of his dealings with women? Is he a debaucher?'

'Let me tell you about his great collection. I am familiar with most of it.'

There were no more than six patients. Although Foart's income was less with so few, his rates were high, five guineas a week. A small number meant a greater chance of cure. Meals were regular, cooked well. Inmates were clean, dressed by nine o'clock; at all meals sat together, conversed rationally.

Edward wouldn't leave his room, wouldn't eat until I persuaded him that appearance of conformity might release him sooner. I went with him to breakfast in a pale green dining-room, its painted panels hung with engravings of mob-capped beauties; large, brown oils of anonymous ancestors. Dr Foart sat at the head of a polished table with plentiful silverware, covered dishes. I stood opposite Edward and wrote down this conversation soon after.

'Mr Gage, we are not quite a full house. But, let me introduce you to James Hadfield, soldier and latterly silversmith; Richard Broughton, preacher, yes, a famous preacher.'

He indicated next an old lady in archaic clothing. Tiny, concentrating on her plate. 'Miss Addison, daughter of the famed writer and editor. And we yet await Mrs Bewdley. Edward Gage has a fine collection, I am told. Mr Sanders is with him temporarily.'

Edward acknowledged each barely. Hadfield groaned, put his hand to his head, began to push back his chair. Scarred across the eye, down one cheek, his expression was fearsome.

'Don't go, Mr Hadfield,' Foart said. 'He has suffered great wounds in the war, you know.'

'Three hours in a ditch. Left for dead. Fought for King and Country. Fifteenth Light Dragoons.' I saw the regimental buttons on his waistcoat.

'It cannot be done,' said Broughton, a smooth man, alight as if addressing an adoring crowd. 'You cannot serve two masters, Hadfield.' Hadfield sat down, groaned again.

'You cannot serve the King *and* the Lord God.' Broughton turned to Edward. 'That's why I left the Royal Navy, Mr Gage. I was a lieutenant. They paid me off handsomely. Left me to do my work here in Babylon.'

'Prisoner of the French,' Hadfield ground his teeth. 'Persecuted. But I have not yet been sufficiently tried. I know what I have yet to endure.'

'The angel never mentioned you to me, Hadfield. In that whole long and lovely address for which I was chosen, I never heard mention of your name. Not once.'

'I have received a divine commission.'

'*I* have received a divine commission.'

'Gentlemen!' Foart said, looking up from his dish of kidneys.

'Ah!' Broughton suddenly exclaimed. 'It is she!' A woman of thirty entered the room, fashionably dressed, her gown gathered under the bosom, hair in the natural style. Smiling, steadying herself on the back of Edward's chair, she sat next to him.

Broughton continued: 'I have been expecting you, heavenly lady! You have brought me love, happiness, riches! Descended from the clouds!'

Hadfield growled. 'Said that yesterday, Broughton.'

Mrs Bewdley took pieces of buttered toast, giggled.

'Mr Broughton, look through the window. It is a sunny day, the sky is cloudless. I have descended from my room by the staircase. Dr Foart, I am sorry to be late once more. The time I need to take the drops!' She murmured to Edward. 'Four hundred drops of laudanum a day you know. There now, what do you think of that? But the time it takes to get it all down!' She smiled at him with the beauty of complete joy.

'We shall reduce that number, Mrs Bewdley,' said Foart, looking hastily at me. 'Management not medicine.'

'Oh no, I don't think so, Doctor. Do you?' Edward didn't answer.

'If you are *not* she, then I shall heal you, dear lady. For the Fall will come. It will come. It has only been postponed for a while. And I hear it. At night I hear it approaching Babylon. Dragging, dragging its great, scaly body. So, *dear* lady, I shall heal you before that dreadful day.'

'You are so kind. But, really, Mr Broughton, I am not in need of healing. As to the Fall with which you threaten us daily, shall I weep or laugh? What say you, Miss Addison?' Mrs Bewdley beamed at the old lady, whose tongue captured crumbs from her tiny fingertips like a chameleon catching flies.

Miss Addison rolled her eyes. 'Tragi-comedy, which is the product of the English theatre, is one of the most monstrous inventions that ever entered into a poet's thoughts. An author might as well think of weaving the adventure of Aeneas and Hudibras into one poem, as of writing such a motley piece of mirth and sorrow.'

'Stop her!' Hadfield urged under his breath at Miss Addison's relentless, tinkling monotone.

'But the absurdity of these performances is so very visible that I shall not insist upon it.'

'She knows her father's works by heart. Every word. Come Miss Addison,' said Dr Foart, 'let me take you upstairs.'

Hadfield, Broughton and Mrs Bewdley fell on the remaining dishes. Edward signed to me and we left the room.

Foart had a botanic garden behind the asylum for the recreation of his patients. He had little success; they saw no point in taking on the work of their inferiors. After I left, Edward, shunning company, agreed to dig the ground, though he would eat the herbs, set traps for birds among the bushes. He told me how Foart found him there, absorbed. How he'd questioned him, elicited nothing. Persisted, broke his own declared intention not to use threats, mentioned the new electrical treatment for melancholy. Left Edward weeping.

Foart believed in the importance of forgetting. When he learned enough for his analysis he decided there was over-exertion of Edward's mental faculties with, he surmised, some disappointment of passion. He must forget Lapland! All objects and books that might remind him were forbidden. The subject must not be discussed. Not that anyone around the table was likely to raise it. Only metropolitan food was provided, dressed, devilled, fricasséed, jellied.

The pistols were Hadfield's. Although forbidden him, since he must forget his attempt on the life of the king, they'd easily been secreted by his old friend Mrs Mason. Hadfield was plotting escape with Broughton and Edward, who borrowed the firearms to practise the hold and feel of them.

I heard what happened from Edward and the doctor both. It seems that in following Crichton's *Inquiry* Foart must go through the exercise of *self-analysis*, to abstract his own mind from himself, place it before him, as it were, and examine it with freedom and impartiality. This he was doing when Edward burst upon him with two cocked pistols.

'Where is my reindeer? You have stolen my little reindeer!'

'Mr Gage, put down the pistols and let us talk together. You know there are no animals in the house. They are not allowed.'

'You've taken my reindeer because you want me to forget. *Forget*, you say. I *cannot*, *will* not forget. It is in your clothing, the reindeer. You've stolen it. Take off your clothes!'

Foart was not within reach of his bell. He took off his well-cut coat. Edward waved a pistol at his stomach.

'Empty the pockets!'

Foart pulled out paper scraps, coins, a box of snuff. He scoffed: 'A reindeer in my pocket!'

'Cameo. Rose-pink agate.' Tears welled. 'You've hidden it in your clothing. Off! Off! Take everything off!'

Foart kicked off his shoes, stripped breeches, stockings, waistcoat, shirt, began to remove the undershirt when his servant stepped into the room behind Edward and snatched the pistols. They were unloaded.

The doctor never used strait-waistcoats. Edward, crushed, was easily locked in his room. Toast and a basin of tea were given but not taken. Crouching on the floor in misery, he found the reindeer cameo under his bed and holding it tight in his fist beat his head against the floorboards in joy and wretchedness.

He was confined for days. When at last I was told, Foart said:

'A case of *hallucinatio maniacalis*. I cannot let him out.'

He rejected my pleas; furibund patients were a danger. Then suddenly he allowed Edward into the garden which was badly in need of weeding. From where, having encouraged him to eat himself back to strength, it was not hard with signals, rope and a waiting trap to have him over the wall.

Once more he roamed his land. Among rocks and bilberries. The magistrate relented, with assurances from me. But Edward was broken. He would not go indoors, for doors could close, be locked. Even near to the house someone might assault him with Babylon, ditches, laudanum, tragicomedy. Electrical treatment to the head.

He moved the tent far into the woods, stoked a continuous fire, dosed himself with brandy, ate meat raw or ashy, blackened in the flames. He would countenance no one, scarcely even me. I kept some watch but wouldn't spy. He knew quite well that nobody would come if the tent caught fire in deep night and cooked him, stupefied, curled like an infant under piles of skins.

I returned to Brighthelmstone. Sold my valuable knife collection, opened a house for so-called lunatics. In Edward's library I'd found Locke's essay. Madmen have not lost their reason, he says, rather, 'having joined together some ideas very wrongly, they mistake them for truths.' My asylum was no Collegium Insanorum. Certainly there were no strait-waistcoats, mechanical aparatus, bleeding, blistering. No well-clad mad-doctors. No self-analysis. Above all, no confinement.

I sought out Maria. The daughter of my employer before Edward. She had chosen to rehabilitate her dead mother's muddied reputation, rather than marry me, her mother's footman. By now her mother was surely forgotten by the world and I had something more to offer her. We could run the place together, treat madmen with understanding, common-sense, kindness.

Approaching her house, I relived her mother's incessant demands, domination. Maria's eager grasp in dark corridors and stairwells. Perhaps she had married, I thought, moved away.

Her mother's portraits covered the walls; her mother's novels filled shelves; her notes, poems, letters were piled in boxes, mounds, scattered over tables, floorboards. Maria sat in her mother's chair, by the window's perfect seascape, stout but recognisable. Looked round at me, her hands scuttering like mice among papers on her lap. Stared, unblinking. Turned back to the sea.

Forgiven

'You'll be dead within the month,' apothecary Sawbridge tells him.

That's how it is with Sawbridge. Their friendship, Harley's only friendship, has grown out of the muck of truth. Has sprung up like rhubarb, bold and sour, its leaves poisonous, its body acidic, curative. They've never lied to each other, never eased discourse with sweet deceit.

Everything is grist: Reform, finally in place, trade unions, Ireland, cursed evangelicals, geology, dissection, Shelley, the railway, God. Sawbridge is moderate; Harley, the school-teacher, still radical. They set out their life-stories like specimens pinned through the heart, to closely scan and criticise. All is admitted, nothing discarded.

For years they argue over the tale of the dog so loyal that it would let no one approach the body of its dead master. Famished, it ate the upper part of the man's face, some of his neck, one of his shoulders. Sawbridge sees it as a simple demonstration of the limitations of the animal mind. Harley insists it is an emblem: the master freedom, dead, the dog revolution, intractably loyal to the concept, able to survive only by doing it violence.

Sawbridge examines Harley, his pulse, tongue, eyeballs, temperature. He listens to rasping breaths through his new stethoscope.

'You might not last a fortnight, Harley.'

'I've been waiting since '95. Thirty-nine years.'

'You know my opinion of that.'

'I do.'

'I shall increase the laudanum.'

'I'm sorry I shan't be there to give your eulogy, doctor to the humble. Sawbridge. Sawbones.'

There's little for Harley to do. He'll tell the Board to advertise for a new teacher. He's already willed his books and rickety spinet to Sawbridge. He's written to his daughter. The first child, a boy, died years ago. He'd left his wife before the girl was born, at the start of the new century. She might want to know why her father moved miles away from London, why they've never known each other. She'll be thirty-four now. Perhaps she will forgive him.

*

The harvest shrivelled in 1794. Then came a freezing winter. Ripples of ice crimped the shores of the Thames, leaving a central channel into which a man, drunk with warming brandy fell, froze to death and floated downstream. Harley provided food and fuel for his wife and baby from his wages as a hairdresser; his wife sewed linen bolster covers. The marriage was an obligation, the baby a sickly, squalling thing that broke the night to pieces.

'My father fought for the king in America,' he tells Sawbridge. 'A lieutenant. What glory! For nine years he sat all day in a chair by the fire with his bloody stump and mad eyes. Never spoke. I was terrified. Yet my mother bore him three more children.

'I was the eldest. When he died I could no longer hide behind the few volumes given me out of pity by the schoolmaster. A hairdresser nearby offered work. I had no choice.

'It seems to me that we powdered every head in the West End. I learned to curl, crimp, frizz, place false hair and hair cushions. I smeared scented pomatum, my fingers dipped in brick dust for the grip, combed, parted, pinned, scraped greasy foreheads with the powder knife and puffed superfine jasmine, attar of roses, heliotrope powder at four shillings a pound.

'I should have put that powder knife to better use. Exchanged the wretched wheat powder for lime.'

But at the start he was fifteen and not oblivious to the exotic charm of dressing rooms off Portman square, to the unblemished beauty of a few, if not all of the powdered, to greedy, flirtatious glances. Lickbarrow his employer, who sometimes called himself Monsieur Lickbarrow, played erotic games with his clients by innuendo, flattery, discreet and indiscreet gestures. In such an atmosphere it was to be expected that Harley would not resist temptation when, after an appointment, he and Lickbarrow were fed and watered below stairs.

He was seventeen when Molly declared him the cause of her expulsion from service. It was then, as they set up home in lodgings off Hedge Street that Harley became radical. A Foxite whose hair he'd been dusting with blue powder noticed him eyeing a pamphlet on the floor of his dressing room and gave it him. Harley learned that he was powdering the hair of the rich with the bread of the poor.

Sleepless from the baby's howling, Harley was nourished by revolutionary air abroad in the streets and at meetings he began to attend. He carried Paine in his coat, was stirred to the core hearing Thelwall. He posted handbills and joined both processions of triumph when Hardy and then Thelwall were acquitted at the Old Bailey. He enjoyed his double life, grooming Tory heads to the inner music of last night's lecture:

'Citizens! . . . the frying pan of despotism . . . king Chaunticleer with his crown, his coxcomb'.

In the spring of '95 Lickbarrow panicked at Pitt's hairpowder tax. Not that the rich couldn't afford to pay their statutory guinea – guinea pigs! – but the moral argument was stronger, would obviously hold sway. Harley's radical friends found him work in a print shop.

While his life as a husband disintegrated into squalor, complaint and recrimination, his mental life grew. He read fervently, talked with a rapid, nervous concision, earned the respect of his fellows.

*

She picks her way through leaning piles of paper. Shelves hold books upright, sideways, pressed into gaps, spilling over the floor. A fold in the turkey carpet almost trips her and she sits after Harley removes a heap of Blackwood's and pulls nervously at the curtains. More light is worse; her fingers twitch with a longing to tidy, sweep, throw out.

Harley coughs. 'It's kind of you to come so far,' and coughs again. It's no wonder, she thinks, with all that dust.

'In your letter you wrote that you had something to say before you die.' No glimmer of emotion in this Ann, the child he'd not cared to know. He sees a stout middle-aged woman, heavily clothed, unsmiling. She takes off her bonnet and gloves but retains her shawl, despite the stuffy warmth. He opens a window and a flock of papers blow onto her lap. July light glares at her embarrassment, her irritated frown.

July spilled heat and blood.

On the 12th of the month, 1795, a fifer told of imprisonment in a crimping house, claimed he'd been chained in a cellar. People ran, broke down the door, destroyed everything; soldiers dispersed them, hauled the fifer off to Newgate. The story was false – it was a public house, the King's Arms; Lewis, the fifer drunk. (Not like the previous summer when George Howe, no older than Harley, escaping crimpers, jumped from a garret window. The image of thin, untried hands tied behind his broken back lived on in Harley's mind.)

Nevertheless, rebellion was abroad. The price of wheat ten shillings and sixpence and rising; a worthless war, calamitous defeats. The crowd, driven from Charing-Cross, smashed Pitt's windows in Downing Street, surged on to St George's Fields, gutted a recruiting house near the obelisk, set fire to furniture. Horse guards were called, the city and borough associations, Lambeth volunteers. A magistrate read the riot act to no effect. Guards galloped into the crowd, trampling, maiming, under arms all night. Harley and his friends joined the throng the following day.

Ann Chance folds her hands and looks at him coldly.

'I may live no more than two weeks, Ann.'

'I am sorry to hear it. Is that what you wanted to say to me?'

'I thought to explain why I left London all those years ago.'

'You abandoned my mother before I was born. Do you hope to right that wrong? It is surely too late.' He admires her reason, notes her refusal to call him Father.

'I cannot right it but I am sorry and ask your forgiveness.'

'Tell me why you left London.' I've made a pointless journey, she thinks.

Harley and his companions merely intended to observe the attack on the Royal George recruitment house. It was evening though not yet dark and the air stank of summer sewers, smouldering wood, burned varnish. The crowd jeered at the soldiers, laughed, bawled news of the wounded to each other. Harley eased his way towards the smashed house. As bedding was thrown onto the road and lit to cheers, more lifeguards and Surrey fencibles arrived. Then three companies of footguard, their hair pulled back, greased, powdered.

A roar of fury leapt through the crowd and Harley, fired by fellow-feeling, trembling with rage, stooped for stones to throw, sticks, horse dung. He hurled a burned chair leg, a brass drawer handle at the mass of soldiers. There was a stirring satisfaction in it. Moving nearer, he saw a man close to the line of lifeguards.

'Pull the reins!' he called to him. 'Pull them towards you!'

The man reached out, horses jostled. Suddenly the lifeguard raised his sword. Harley picked up a brick and threw it hard, saw it strike the lifeguard, draw blood.

The moment joy surged through him the sword came down and sliced off the hand clutching the reins. In the tableau he'd never erased from memory, Harley saw the man gape in disbelief at his handless wrist, the horse rear then trample him as the guard brought down the forelegs.

Harley looks at his daughter. This woman with lines of impatience at the corners of her mouth.

'In 1795 I was a radical.'

'Radical!' She pulls her shawl about her, protecting herself from him. 'I was born in 1800. You surely need not tell me about 1795.'

Oh reason not the need!

The crowd around him pressed forward, huzzaing and crying 'shame!' at the lifeguards. No one noticed how Harley stood apalled. No one knew which missile he had thrown. He saw a body carried away. Later he thought to ask at St Martin's bone house, but hadn't the courage to find the name.

For five years Harley lived in half-light. He'd not killed the man yet he had caused his death. He told neither wife nor companions of his torment, fearing their excuses, their easy attribution of blame elsewhere. He shrank into himself. His companions thought his sensibility too great and knew, also, of the burden of his marriage. For the baby, unwanted, resented, had died and Molly strayed, returned and strayed again.

With Pitt's terror, open meetings were abandoned though the friends met and drank together. Danger touched them all when Hadfield, one of their group, made an attempt on the king's life. Harley drugged himself with books, hiding in the authority of print. Clothed himself in consoling pedantry.

One day near the St Giles rookeries he saw the man. He knew him by his single hand and from his expression which still registered astonishment, overlaid by pain and despair. His legs were bent inwards from the knees, crimpled, his feet turned towards each other, his walk a mockery.

Harley went up to him.

'Sir. A word with you, please!' The man, whose eyes were fixed on the path, on how to remain upright upon it, shambled off.

'Sir! I beg of you. Let me speak.' The man half turned, waved his handless arm in Harley's face.

'Hear me, sir,' Harley pleaded. Staring up at him, shaking, the man groaned from a profound inner pit of misery. Then he twisted precariously, stumbled along the street, hauled himself up some steps, leaning exhausted against the frame as he unlocked the door.

For Harley leaving London was not flight. His actions in the riot had ruined the cripple's life. His own life appeared to him a series of random states – his work, his marriage, his encounter with radicals. He would take himself in hand, act only with purpose, make all well. A border land seemed suitable. Remote. Bleak.

His resolve began badly. Lately he had taken Molly back in bitter charity. As he packed his box with papers, books and five patched shirts, he knew that she was expecting his child. He asked her to come with him, knowing she would not and later, in the blue-slated school-house received her letter about the birth of his daughter.

'Very well, then. I'll begin in 1800.'

'Why did you leave?'

'I caused harm to someone, unintentionally. I resolved to live a better life.'

'You caused harm to my mother by leaving her.'

'Your mother preferred to remain in London. I sent her regular payments to keep you clothed and fed until such time as you might marry.'

'That was the least you could do.'

'Indeed it was. Understand that our marriage barely existed. Before your birth your mother was unfaithful to me. We were not happy. Not ever.'

She reddens and looks down. 'She is dead and cannot defend herself.'

'It was not Molly I left so much as my life in London. I came here to do some good; to teach the young.'

'You chose children who were nothing to you over your own child.'

'I'm sorry that I was no father to you, Ann. Even if you cannot understand, can you not forgive me?'

She stares at the violet silk of her skirt. Sun no longer burns through the angled panes.

He relieves her.

'I have lived a quiet life.' He waves his hand around the room, stirring up dust, coughs. 'I have little to leave. Do you have children, Ann?' She stiffens at the use of her name once more. 'And your husband …?'

'We have no children. Mr Chance has a very successful business – he is the most important mercer in Reading. We have four servants and our own coach and pair.'

'You will be remembered in my will, nonetheless.'

*

Sawbridge's eulogy for Harley is short; the funeral attended by few mourners. Mrs Chance is not among them.

Sawbridge knows but doesn't speak of Harley's thirty-nine years of expiation. He doesn't say that their friendship was Harley's principle comfort. Had he been a priest Sawbridge would have offered God's mercy, but neither man believed. What Sawbridge offered was reason, patience, truth; with these Harley's torment had lessened. He had been a good teacher. His pupils remembered him: too young to notice his radical views, old enough to feel his kindness.

As he boxes up the books, treading delicately between piles of pamphlets, Sawbridge thinks of Mrs Chance, described by his friend shortly before his death. How will she react to her solicitor's letter with its enclosure of four pounds? With a tightening of the lips, a gasp of disgust.

Harley always knew that his deepest need must be denied him. Thomas Skelton of 17 Dyott Street, St.Giles's-in-the-Fields receives his final monthly payment, greatly more than usual, without having discovered the name of his benefactor, without having forgiven.

SHRIVEN

It was over in eight minutes: catlin cut through skin and flesh, arteries ligatured, smashed humerus sawn, stump below shoulder cauterised. Gently he pressed more rum through the young man's lips, helped friends carry him to bed.

Swiftly, cleanly done. A life saved. So far. He knew how infection might strike in days, how even recovered there was no work for a labourer with one arm. He'd saved him for a life of bleakness.

Surgeon-apothecary Sawbridge was renowned for miles both sides of the border. From hill to receding hill. His immaculate surgery was rarely used. He set bones, pulled teeth, lanced boils, distributed draughts, instructions. Received little payment; persuaded the poor that vaccination wouldn't turn them into cows. Was renowned for his skill but also for his kindness conveyed through touch, expression, tender inclination of his body rather than words. His patients were humble, lives narrowed by necessity, afflicted by accident. What use were words to them?

Countless deliveries, babies alive, dead, whole, unformed; mothers encouraged, fathers consoled. They wondered why he'd never married, had children of his own. His delicacy with women, his sweet way with children who obeyed, never screamed, adored him, raised the same comment – what a good husband he'd make, what a good father. Until age changed the tense of the verb.

He had little time for marriage perhaps. His patients, spread widely, had large families in small spaces, hard lives in fields, woods, on freezing hillsides. Often he rode out, returned late. Then Harley came to the blue-slated school house, escaping disaster in London. A friendship struck that lived for almost forty years. Answered some need in each, dwelling as it did in honesty and acceptance. Normally spare of speech, Sawbridge opened up to Harley whose mental sufferings he tended. They exposed their lives to each other, peered, poked about, retrieved deep-lodged shards. Harley's life was more complex. Heavy, festering guilt required constant recitation at first. Later he complained that Sawbridge made light of the disappointment in his own life.

Sawbridge's apprenticeship had begun with placing leeches, pounding powders, holding bowls when blood was let. A silent boy. Witness to small and great suffering. An uncle funded a bout of study in London to improve on this rural round. Up and down the spiral staircase at St Thomas's he went to watch and learn the newest ways in surgery. Filled a stack of notebooks from lectures on anatomy, chemistry, physiology. Uneasy in the city he did little else but work. Back home among clouded hills, drab chapels, he began the practice that created so much local glory and puzzlement.

One of his patients was a small landowner whose family suddenly sprouted illness. Charmed by Sawbridge's medical confidence and apparent political reticence, the landowner invited him to attend bedsides and social events equally. To use the library freely, though he hardly had the leisure for it.

Unlike Harley's experience with women, carnal, disastrous, Sawbridge saw the landowner's daughter Laetitia and loved her straight away. She was sixteen, too young, but he could wait. He made no promises to himself, employed no visions. Observed; savoured proximity whenever it occurred. Watched her eat, dance, sing, chatter in a way delightfully alien to him. Sometimes walking, they became separated from the rest, ambled together among clusters of marble shepherds, shepherdesses, lines of tender exotic trees. Once he made a pencil sketch which he kept, folded, next to his heart and showed to Harley some twelve years into their friendship.

'Only *now* you show me this vital piece of yourself! I'm offended.'

'Nonsense! You know the story,'

'But you *still* keep it next to your heart, Sawbridge.'

'I'm a man of habit.'

'Tell me again why you didn't marry her?'

'It wasn't clear that my feelings were reciprocated.'

She married the eldest son of a neighbouring baronet, lived in a fine house not far away. Sawbridge attended her first two births; struggled to save her before the grand physician arrived from London for the third.

Now, Harley was dying.

'No vicar, no preacher!' he reminded Sawbridge.

'You know, people often confess at the end, believers or no. Even confess themselves to *me*.'

'That's no surprise. There's that about you, my friend. You're like sunlight breaking through a dark wood – people turn to you, give themselves up to you. Look at me. What *haven't* I told you about myself? I am fully shriven. But it doesn't work the other way round. I've had to squeeze with all my might to get a drop from you. In another life you'd have been a priest.'

'And who will shrive me?'

'Surely *you've* nothing to confess? Your life's been a simple, daily heroism.'

'No more than Amos dragging lambs out of ewes in a snowdrift.'

Harley's protest was lost in coughing that racked him; gasping, retching, he was too weak for further argument.

Sawbridge gave Harley a month. Harley could no longer teach but it was summer and there was no hurry for him to vacate the school house. How often had they planned new worlds together among leaning towers of books: *The Rights of Man*, *The Necessity of Atheism*, a heap of Cobbett's *Political Register* balancing on a *Pilgrim's Progress* supported by three volumes of D'Oyley and Mant. Now they sat sweating by Harley's fire, banked up despite the heat, Sawbridge in shirtsleeves, Harley shivering in coat and blanket.

'I do have something to tell you if you'll hear me. I have kept this back from you even while you told me everything.'

'I forgive you for that, Sawbones.' They laughed, Harley with pain.

'I'd delivered several babies by the time Laetitia had her first confinement,' Sawbridge began. He hadn't found it difficult clearing out the crowd of female midwives and friends, he said, who in those days, fussing like geese, attended every birth from the highest to the lowest, excluding fresh air and men from wherever the birth took place.

He'd seen little of her since her marriage. Wasn't welcome as he had been at her father's. Her husband avoided him, employed him only when he had to, saw him as a purveyor of pills.

She was very frightened, shocked, unwilling to take much brandy. Sawbridge held her hand, encouraged her, even tried to divert her with memories of events in her recent girlhood at which he'd been present.

Her husband rode out on all these occasions so that when a fever set in after the third, premature birth, he was not to be found for several hours. As her mind began to wander, Sawbridge stroked her arm, felt her frenzied pulse against his wrist. Fragments of her life broke out without boundaries of time. She called for her dead father, gave household orders, sang childish songs, muttered prayers, all tangled with each other. Lay still. Flamed up again. Turned suddenly to Sawbridge, pulled at his shirt with extraordinary force.

'You never said! You never asked me!' Hectic, glittering, she began to whistle, fell asleep.

'I got her through it. I've no idea why she survived. Couldn't account for it then, can't now.' She was well, if weak, in time for the appearance of the husband and the grand physician. He was not asked to attend the family again.

'I resumed work and at first spent little time thinking about what she'd said. Yet it crept into my heart and hid there.'

'Lived like a toad crouching at the bottom of the cistern.'

'I like toads.'

'You let her slip away.'

'Yes.' The April day among bluebells under oak trees, when he helped adjust her shawl against still lingering chill. When somehow the moment passed.

'Sawbridge, it was your own fault you lost her.'

'Yes, it was.' Condemned himself to a life of bleakness.

'And she lost you. What was *her* life? Tolerable of course. Not happy. But how can I absolve you?'

He helped Harley to bed, went home. Realised how over the years, after rehearsing again and again his fatal involvement in the riot of 1795, Harley had gradually calmed. He had reviewed his life, struggled to understand his failings, motives; succeeded. He was ready to die.

Sawbridge was hale, strong, yet he had no knowledge of himself. *Why* did he let the most important things pass by? Why had he left it till now to tell Harley what Laetitia had said in her delirium? Was it reticence or cowardice? Was reticence cowardice? It was too late for Harley to help him find answers. And if Harley could also not absolve him he must remain unshriven.

Cholera lashed the country. Only coffin-makers flourished. Laetitia, a middle-aged widow in her newly gothicised, battlemented house died along with her two older children; as did so many of the poor in their insanitary shacks by the common-sewer stream.

Sawbridge is seventy, vigorous if somewhat stiff in the mornings, misses Harley, attends all sufferers as often as ever. Rides along lanes, up steep tracks beyond battered hawthorn. Laetitia's nineteen-year-old daughter, Frances, with the old wise eyes of the prematurely born, sick with disease and terror of death, having watched her mother and siblings die, survives, and in relief and gratitude accepts Sawbridge's offer of marriage.

There is brief disgust at this action – the prudery of a small rural town – though it soon dissipates. The people are too fond of their surgeon-apothecary for it to last. The accusation that he's married for money is groundless, since he insists he and his wife live as he's always done in his modest grey-brick villa. There are no children. Frances learns to scrub instruments, hold bandages for the dressing of ulcers, soothe colic, clean bloody limbs.

The first April, Sawbridge and his wife walk in the grounds of her house, shuttered, emptied. They stop to observe oak buds breaking out, bluebells soon to uncurl. She sits on a stone bench and is startled to find him on his knees in last year's leaves, grasping her hand. He tells of his great, enduring love for her mother, of Laetitia's exclamations after giving birth to her.

Her existence shakes; and yet she feels relief, is glad. Understands. Consoles. Helps him up, his shrift complete.

FROM THE LIFE

The accident changed everything. At first, when he couldn't walk without crutches, Digham made up a truckle bed for him in a cupboard off the printing room, where he'd sleep until he could take the stairs and return to his lodgings in Albion Place. This might seem like excessive kindness on the part of a master for his apprentice, but Digham knew the value of Joseph Young's work and couldn't do without him.

Besides, a bond had formed between the two over almost seven years. Age, temperament, experience, politics, status, even size stood between them but were smothered by mutual respect. Joseph watched with awe William Digham's rapid strokes with the etching needle; his witty put-downs of the Prince of Wales's foibles and excesses, of ministers and their latest mistresses, the ridiculous ferocity of the French. William in turn admired Joseph's engraving, the subtle variation of angles at which the young man pushed the burin's lozenge-shaped point, his concentration no less than obsession. Together they produced satires sold in the shop below that amused, provoked, avoided prosecution.

'What is *this*?'

Digham stood beneath lines of damp prints drying like washing on a breezeless day. A little man, his baldness warmed by a felt hat, he peered at a sheet through thick lenses.

That Joseph's apprenticeship was almost at an end didn't mean he should make no effort, Digham remarked.

'Whose idea have you etched so miserably? I need no counterproof to see that it has come out vilely.'

Etching and engraving puny satires drawn by rich customers brought needed income.

'That's just it, sir. The *idea* is miserable; a paltry Tory jibe. It doesn't deserve reproduction. It should be thrust in the fire.'

The two men were so politically opposed that there were times when even copying Digham's own designs carefully onto copper was distasteful to Joseph. Yet at least Digham's ideas were conceived with humour and drawn with great skill.

'We are being *paid*, Young. If Lady Parrot's notion is feeble that is too bad. Your opinion is not part of the arrangement. You must do it again. Same plate – we can't afford a new one. Burnish off these parts, deepen the lines round the figures.'

Joseph sighed, began to rub the burnisher over the plate.

'Or is it the ankle? Does it still hurt after your mysterious accident about which you've told us nothing? But, good Lord, an ankle's little enough use in engraving!

'Keep your Jacobin sympathies under your hat, young man Young,' Digham concluded, looking over his spectacles at his doodling, dreaming apprentice, whose long legs stuck out awkwardly from under the bench. 'When you set up on your own you'll see how far you get with those opinions.'

Digham barely concealed from himself a doubt that Young's dreamy, idealistic character would produce satires with any force. It was all very well having your head full of Milton all day. He read too much, his coat pockets baggy with books.

Digham felt a one-sided affection for the young man who'd come to him educated, precocious, withdrawn. When Mrs Young died suddenly, Joseph's silk mercer father broke down, was bankrupt within a year and apprenticed the fourteen-year-old to Digham. The boy had shown himself good at drawing; his father couldn't afford to keep him. He'd learned fast, become an excellent engraver. As long as he worked for Digham he was secure. But the older man nurtured a dread of letting him go. Surely, he'd founder without knowledge of the world.

The star-wheel creaked. Batley bent his knee to push one spike, pulled another with his podgy arms. The pressman had worked for Digham for forty years. Digham looked again at Joseph staring through the lattice. Light in the printing room shone pond-green from a tree dense with new leaves.

It was quite by chance that at seventeen Joseph heard courageous John Thelwall speak and found more than he'd lost when his childhood collapsed: feeling, inspiration, idealism.

'I affirm that *every* man and *every* woman and *every* child ought to obtain something more than food and rags and a wretched hammock with a poor rug to cover it without working twelve or fourteen hours a day. They have a claim, a sacred and inviolable claim.'

How they cheered in the packed hall! And Pitt brought in a gagging act just for Thelwall.

Weekly, Joseph paid his penny to the London Corresponding Society, met the fellows in his division and was constantly stirred. He pasted bills with pot and brush, graduated to writing pamphlets, read and read, sharpening his ambition to move the crowd with his own oratory.

He'd broken his ankle on the day of the bread riot. Shamefully, slipping in hot dung, knocked by a carriage. Not hurling brickbats, stones; not crying out with the rest. Not even anywhere near them. No one knew the true story, but as soon as the ankle had mended he resumed his attendance at his division, anxious to assuage guilt and shame.

He offered to write up the next bill for printing then found he was arguing against too many bills.

'It's no use,' he said. 'There's such a quantity of bills posted everywhere – the public will not look at them!'

Irritation with his fellow members pricked him like a rash. Too much noise at meetings. Too much reporting to and from the General Committee. The president and secretary both more finicky than the most crabbed of pedants.

Each division must debate what was debated by each *other* division. Equality was thoroughgoing in the Society. Impatient with the laborious procedure, he was no longer stirred, when once the very utterance of certain phrases had moved him to tears. He began to sense a dislocation from his fellow Citizens, dyers, china-burners, wire-workers, locksmiths, sucking earnestly on their pipes.

Perhaps it was the humiliation. For there had been that, too, as well as shame. Insensible after the collision, he'd been taken into a House, a superior whorehouse near St James's where he'd wandered, drawn to the seat of power. There he was sneered at by its renowned owner whose carriage had injured him, a woman whose features he recognised from having engraved a series of Digham's satires. It was a place where corruption and vice were of the highest order and he couldn't run from it! Had been forced to remain and be laughed at.

Shame, humiliation. His thoughts hobbled, confused.

*

One night, he and other members arriving early are confronted by the landlord of the Angel where the division meets.

'You must move yourselves to an upper bedroom. I have a meeting of the Society of Loyal Britons to accommodate,' the man tells them, looking anywhere but into their eyes.

They know at once he means to get them out, has probably been threatened by the justices. Throughout the meeting, squeezed into an unsuitable attic, the committee seated neatly round the edge of the stained bed, a loud roar of meaty men bawling *God Save the King*, *Rule Britannia*, *Britons Strike Home* and such like assails them.

Propelled by loathing, Joseph agrees to find another meeting place and goes straight to the Bricklayers' Arms where, relieved at making an arrangement with the landlord, he takes a second drink.

Through the ceiling comes the sound of music. The normally abstemious Joseph has a momentary shock. He thinks he hears again an exquisite voice singing an aria in Italian – his first experience of rapture. For shame had been followed by humiliation, humiliation by rapture. Immobile in a place no better than hell, he'd suddenly heard anguish expressed as pure beauty. All previous thought was re-etched, fine lines erased, grooves filled with copper burr. The song cut as deep as the steel could go. It rang in black lines over and over again, possessing his mind.

But no, it isn't that voice, that song; yet it is a woman's voice and he follows it without hesitation through the fug of pipe smoke, stench of cheese, along rush-lit passages, up stairs. There in the rowdy crowd he pays his four pence for music and a girl, beer, punch and tobacco extra, and arrives at Digham's the next morning late and bleary.

Digham remonstrates, threatens, doesn't demand an explanation. Guesses and is glad.

The apprenticeship is over. Digham continues to employ Joseph as an engraver until he can afford to set up on his own. He tolerates the young man's dissoluteness, for his work, however late in the day he produces it, is excellent. Joseph frequently attends the Bricklayers' cock and hen club from which no one leaves alone and whose raucous activities provoke raids by the constables. The sketchbook in his coat is full of drawings. In time he pairs up with the singer. She is known best for her rendering of the old song *Sandman Joe*, rotating breasts and hips to make her listeners roar with lascivious pleasure.

The disembodied voice of a whore singing *Lascia ch'io pianga* beats like blood at the back of his head.

Digham holds a print out at arm's length. Batley, sweating, rests on a stool in the corner. In the heat, the lattice has been flung open to cesspool and blossom.

'Could land you in trouble, young man Young.' For *Treason* he's etched a saucy, youthful John Bull aiming sturdy buttocks at a poster of the King, firing a fart in his face. Lively strokes, brisk, bold, ebullient.

'But I see you save your skin with a Pitt-like onlooker accusing our stout Bull of treason. A forceful satire. Ask five shillings for it.

'And *this* print? My! So different. My! How well you've used stipple and aquatint. Wonderful effect.' He takes it to the window. Pores over it.

A woman laments in a garden; a figure of tragic beauty among weeping trees. Done with tenderness, startling.

'Quite remarkable, my friend, and surely from the life,' he says, convinced.

'From *my* life, William,' replies Joseph. 'And not for sale.'

An Experiment: Above

She stood just inside the room, diminutive, her dress too big, drab against polished mahogany. Unaccustomed shoes. She was six; ten days ago he'd sent a ha'penny for her birthday. She replaced her brother in the weekly task, an older boy increasingly surly.

He beckoned her to where he sat, looking through the great south window: his young *magnolia virginiana* not yet flowering. Beyond the garden, fields, sheep-strewn hills.

'You've come to collect the money, Mary. Do you prefer Polly? I've heard your mother call you that.'

'Yes.'

'Do you know my name? You should address me by my name.' His tone was kindly.

'Mr. Powyss.'

'Good. And do you know why I give you this money, Polly?'

'So's we eat more. So's we eat more. Mr Powyss.'

Sudden sunlight lit her face. Round, placid, unresentful. Barely curious. He saw her mother in her; fled the thought.

He put the money in her drawstring purse, watched her unlatch the wicket, run, stop, dawdle on the path towards home.

He felt glad. Turned back to his room: books, engravings, precious Apulian vases. Set of globes. Newly-made cabinet with sloping top, thin wide drawers, for his plans. Necessities of intellect and wealth. He focused on the page before him; fought off a surge of dismay.

Moreham House, 14th June, 1797

Dear Philip,

Warlow's child Mary now comes to collect the money. She's a sweet girl of six and it cheers me to think I'm providing for her among the others. All the children look healthier than they did four years ago, even if they still resist shoes.

Sometimes when I write to you, my friend, I understand how it feels to be a papist making confession! You ask if I consider my action purely good.

He laid down his pen, put away the unfinished letter, rang for Stephens.

'Dust is gathering on the shelves and objects, Stephens.'

'Samuel doesn't like that end of the room, sir.'

'Tell him he must see to it or be replaced.'

'No replacements around here, Mr Powyss, sir.'

He went out to the hothouse. Built to his own design, nine foot wide, sixty foot long, heated by sea-coal boiler five months of the year. His senses rippled like cat's fur. Cucumbers doing well. Melons, new this year, still small but promising. Bunches of tiny grapes, acid-green.

Production was far in excess of need since he never entertained. He compelled the servants to eat pumpkins and rare vegetables. Production was not the point. What mattered was ascertaining the right conditions, recording:

balance of soil, quantity of water, degrees of heat. Like the best gardeners he kept a calendar from year to year. Checked Miller's *Dictionary*.

After six weeks the child had lost her shyness.

'Here you are again, Polly. Did they give you something in the kitchen?'

'Yes. Tea. Piece of bacon.' She picked her teeth.

'Did Catherine take tea leaves out of the pear-wood caddy? It looks like a big pear.'

'Yes. Catherine said I'm a poor wee thing. It's not true because you gives us money. She says because of father.'

'What do *you* say about your father, Polly?'

'He's gone away. Is he dead?'

'What do you think, Polly?'

'Dead, I think.'

'Don't trouble yourself with any more thinking. Take the money to your mother and be kind to her and all your brothers and sisters.'

'Yes, Mr. Powyss.'

Again he watched her innocence. How she brushed the scented peas with her fingers on her way to the gate.

He took out the letter, dipped his pen. Once, half-seriously, his old friend had accused him of amorality. Plants were neither good nor bad, caused no dilemmas of conscience.

> *Perhaps there cannot be a human act of pure goodness.*
> *Such acts are for God alone. We do good as far as we*
> *are able. But remember, this is an experiment. I mean*
> *it to answer to both charity and science.*

The child must remain in ignorance. He'd speak to the servants. Their restlessness was increasing. He would not be coerced into paying them more.

Worse, there'd been sounds. Distant but discernible. He'd keep talking when the child was there so she'd not hear.

Your final question is more difficult to answer. Of course ill could come out of a good act. But surely it would be inadvertent. No one can intend both good and ill. That defies logic.

He wouldn't tell Philip about Hannah. Warlow's wife. He'd certainly not intended what came about. Yet he could not call it ill. It was she who'd come for the money at first, her baby left with the oldest child – there were eight of them. She'd been shy, but accepted the money without question. As with Polly, no resentment. She was grateful, then awed and, he realised, relieved. He perceived something of what she had endured. Warlow was a big man, wilful, barely articulate, his movements propelled by bulk. Kindness not a quality he understood, so that she turned to it like light. Thin, tendril arms winding, fingers reaching up for life.

Only he and she knew; he believed the servants didn't. Caution made him ask her to send a child for the money instead, to keep encounters rare. His upbringing told him what they did was wrong. His reason, that tenderness was a virtue.

For years he'd cared only for plants. In the garden hollyhocks were shooting up ready to flower, purple *verbena bonanensis* and sweet mauve heliotrope already out – well-established purchases from Chelsea. Cat's Head apples flourishing.

Polly became conversational. She was learning her alphabet at school; he encouraged her, wrote words, drew pictures. H was for holly or Herbert, his name, Hannah, her mother's; I for ivy, J for Jack, her brother, K for king.

'Jack says damn to the king.'

'How old is Jack?'

'Fourteen. He says father said it and father is right.'

'Jack will get into trouble if he says such things. Don't tell anyone else, Polly. It'll do no harm to tell me.'

'Mother says you're good. Jack says damn to Mr Powyss, too.'

'Who is right, do you think?'

'Mother of course! Jack is bad. He hits me.'

'Enough now. On your way.'

It was not extraordinary that a fourteen-year-old boy of almost no education should spout against the monarchy. Liberty was in the air, wherever you looked. Found inscribed on the Market Cross together with 'equality'. Only weeks ago magistrates dispersed a Disputing Club in an ale-house a mile away.

Philip had sent a sixpenny *Rights of Man*, determined to shake him up. He'd not cut the pages. Not that he countenanced hostility. He'd never pay men ten shillings and sixpence to carry Tom Paine's effigy about and shoot at it. He preferred to avoid disruption in his life. Yet already he realised that his best new plants came from America, that radical land: delicate *dodecathon meadia, ceanothus americanus*. The proud juniper that withstood last winter's intense freeze.

He thought he heard movement. The child had gone. He locked the door, knelt on an Ottoman prayer rug at the end of the room near piles of papers. Lifted a sheaf from the floor. Put his ear to the hole.

Thud of clogs on flags. Monotonous, obsessive mumbling passed beneath, moved away out of hearing.

Samuel had drilled two-inch holes in the floorboard and the cellar ceiling. The house was older than it looked from its light-loving façade. Powyss had imposed reason on it years before, upon inheritance. Behind were thick stone walls and foundations out of which cellars had been gouged. Samuel needed help to drill the hollow through which a copper tube would conduct sound from below to the hole under the paper. The hole in the cellar ceiling was unnoticeable: a knot-hole.

That was four years ago, when the advertisement was published, the offer made; made, he'd assured Philip, with the best of intentions. Something he'd read made him ponder for days about the nature of human endurance. About solitariness free from the burden of punishment. Hermits chose to live for years alone, after all. He determined to carry out an experiment, write a full account, publish it.

Was it *so* unreasonable? To see if a man could exist without the comfort of others? Others often provided no comfort. His own life was unsociable, his principal friendship conducted on paper. Weeks passed when he spoke to no one except Stephens, then barely. Felt closer to his new, blue-flowered *lupinus nootkatensis*, whose growth he recorded in a vigorous hand. With books, music, resources of the mind, one surely could exist alone.

A reward of fifty pounds a year for life, the advertisement read, was offered for any man who would undertake to live for seven years underground without seeing a human face, without speaking to a soul.

The only man to respond was Warlow. In a burst of lucidity he said he cared not for human faces, would be glad to be shut of them. For seven years? Yes. Nor was he troubled by the other conditions: to let toe and fingernails grow during the whole of his confinement, together with his beard.

By now he would be shaggy, clawed. But requests were allowed. He had only to ring a bell and barely literate notes were hauled up on the dumb-waiter. Daily ringing signalled removal of his night soil. His clothes were washed on occasion, new ones provided. He'd asked for larger clogs.

Powyss had carefully prepared the underground 'apartments' before he knew who their occupant would be. Under the ballroom – shuttered, untouched – several unused cellars extended to just below the far end of his library. He'd equipped them with good furniture, matting, rugs, oil lamps, books. *Candide*, *Robinson Crusoe*, Defoe's *Journal of a Plague Year*, *The Tempest*, Ferguson's *Astronomy Explained upon Sir Isaac Newton's Principles and made easy to those who have not studied Mathematics.* A cold bath, a chamber organ. Provisions served from his own table sent down three times a day.

For Warlow, a labourer with eight children, here was space unknown, the calm of responsibilities removed, luxury. Time's oppression, invasions of vermin. The company of insects.

At first Powyss had noted down each demand, what was eaten, what left. Warlow wouldn't touch venison, sauces or pickles. Ice-cream returned uneaten, a pool of scummy cream in a dish. He'd listened for every sound. There was little. One day a few notes from the organ. Warlow couldn't play. Whistling that suddenly ceased. Smell of oil smoke from the lamps came up through the hole; the tobacco he'd asked for. Powyss recorded. Sent periodic accounts to Philip.

At some point Warlow began to talk to himself. For months there was intermittent muttering. Then outbursts. Shouts. Thumps. Wild yells. Great shatter of sound as he smashed the organ's keyboard with his fists, arms or what? Powyss imagined the man, huge, bear-headed, howling amid heaps of books he couldn't read. Weeks of silence.

Moreham House, 20ᵗʰ August, 1797

Dear Philip,

Don't imagine I haven't thought about Warlow, even though it's hard to enter the mind of a man with no learning. I do sometimes hear complaining sounds from below, let me tell you, my friend, and these disturb me deeply. But, he agreed to it. Nor has he ever asked to be brought out. And his wife and children are now well fed and clothed (as is he).

Unkindly, you suggest I'm like the man who found a gold ring in a turnip in Northallerton. It is surely Warlow who has found the ring.

These days he rarely completed a letter to Philip. He hated the sight of his complacency spreading like grey mould across the page. He took up the newspaper, read of sea battles with the French and Spaniards; the Thunder bomb, mutiny, violent riot at Tranent.

Escaped to the long south-facing wall where espaliered Ribston pippins began to glow. He pocketed some blemished fruit with which to reprimand Price. Flowerheads heaved with bees and hoverflies.

Polly had begun to read. Powyss was pleased with her. He realised she was never fearful, hadn't learned anxiety. He'd lectured the servants, insisted they give her no hint. They complied but grew sour. Warlow's proximity – one staircase and a nailed-up door were all that separated him from kitchen, pantries, sculleries – made it hard for them to ignore his presence.

Powyss looked forward to Fridays, ink and paper ready. He rewarded each advance by showing her a curio, allowing her to handle it, telling her its story. He watched her when she came and when she left, how she'd find some gaudy flower, touch it, set off its scent. Saw her in his window-framed landscape of garden, fields, hills.

Today, a perfect ammonite lay on his desk.

She broke out as soon as he greeted her.

'My father's in this house! In prison!'

'Who says so, Polly?'

'Catherine.'

'What else does Catherine say?'

'She says he's mad. What *is* "mad"? She says you give money so mother be's quiet. She says it's not fair we have clothes and food and others have none.'

Her look was frank. She expected the truth from him, was amazed he'd been deceptive. He felt a sensation not experienced since childhood. Blushed with shame.

Stumbled to explain. Yes, her father did indeed live in the house, though neither as prisoner nor mad, that he'd agreed to live on his own as an experiment. He would go home in three years, he said and then they'd all have new clothes and plenty of food for the rest of their lives.

She couldn't comprehend 'experiment'.

The image of her face, furious, unfazed by his authority, blazed in his mind.

His equanimity broke.

He walked with Mrs Warlow in his garden, fully visible to the servants.

'I shall free your husband.' *Aster, coreopsis, phlox paniculata*. Red and pink, late summer's blood and flesh.

She shrank as from a blow. Clasped her arms against her ribs.

'I see you don't want that, Hannah.'

'No, sir.'

'Herbert, not 'sir'. No one can hear us. The experiment was wrong. I thought of Warlow as an object to observe, like a plant. I wanted to see how he'd survive in certain conditions. Didn't think he might suffer. He should return and your old life resume.'

'Old life?'

'The agreement would be broken, of course. I could no longer support you. If I did, everyone around would make a claim.'

'The children are well. They will be poor again.'

'And I have taken advantage of you, Hannah.' *Rudbeckia*, black-eyed.

'I am yours.'

He went to the hothouse to think. Melon leaves shrivelled in the heat, their great growth over. He cleared spent cucumber haulm. The experiment was utterly ill-conceived, the results blurred by his selfishness. He needed to cut it down, clear out the wayward growth.

The night's expected storm was violent. Hail stones

shattered the lower lights of the hothouse. The valley would be flooded. He abhorred superstition, thought, with Voltaire, that God cared no more for us than a captain for the mice on his ship. Yet, he'd known so much joy. Fondness for Hannah and Polly, *convolvulus*, grew new blooms daily. Smothering all beneath.

He would release Warlow at midday. Instruct Catherine to pack two baskets with provisions, find work for him for a month or so.

A letter arrived from Philip.

> *You no doubt realise that when the time comes, Warlow may not return gladly to his previous position after so much meat and fish! Have you thought how his bruised children may hate you for releasing him?*
>
> *But you have raised them above their lowly state. Relieved Mrs Warlow of her 'slavery of fear'. We should attend to the rights of woman as to those of man. The spirit of God lives in each person, but in this case the advantages for eight children and their mother far outweigh seven years of minor deprivation for their father. Greater good thus drowns out evil.*
>
> *You joke that I'm your conscience, Herbert. I commend your experiment.*

Reason's clean cut. Just when he'd begun to succumb to a desire for reprobation; to burn before the fiery glance of a child.

Of course, Philip's balance might shift if he learned all. But Powyss knew that the strangely moving exertion of tenderness towards Hannah, the pleasing nurture of Polly could only be weighed with the good.

'Here we are again, Polly! Which flowers did you look at in the garden on your way here?'

'Big, red daisy flowers, Mr Powyss. I likes them.'

So much would flourish. There was yet his paper on the nature of human endurance – his contribution to knowledge. Warlow would be spoken of when he came to light.

He must remain below. The experiment would continue until its end.

Polly would come; encouraged by her mother she would trust him again. There remained the matter of noise, its erratic disturbance. How to prevent her suddenly hearing her father bellow.

He instructed Stephens to move his desk, cabinet and most-used books upstairs to the small sitting-room. The view from the window was less good. He'd have to stand to watch the child against the backdrop of fields and hills. But he could still observe the magnolia, note date and conditions each year when its first buds opened, creamy with promise.

An Experiment: Below

Powyss showed him round. He was proud of the 'apartments'. 'Commodious' the advertisement said. He'd had to ask Powyss what that meant. Two big rooms, furniture, cupboards, bed. No windows. Not this far down. Powyss strode about. Waved his hands.

'Look, Warlow, you're provided with plenty of fuel, kindling. Candles, oil-lamps, tinder-box,' he said.

Table, white cloth, knife and fork. Silver. Glinting in the light from his lamp. Padded chair with carved legs. Pictures on the walls. Looking-glass.

'We'll eat the same food, but yours will come down on the dumb-waiter. Open the hatch. There: two shelves enough for small trays. It's a long way down but with covers the food should remain hot. Pull this cord to send back empty dishes. Ring the bell first.'

Then the organ.

'You keep pumping with your feet while you play. See?'

'Couldn't never learn that.'

'Try, Warlow! There's a box of music: Handel, hymns. Of course I didn't know who would take up the offer. Here's a bath. Ewer, soap – Military Cake, nothing too perfumed. Tooth-brush, powder. The water's cold but it's not far from the fire. The cistern's over there to the side. You could keep an eye on it.'

'Bath?'

'You'll want to wash yourself even if there's no one to see you. Your beard and hair will grow long. Remember? No cutting. No scissors, no razor. Send up your dirty linen. Send up your pot from the close-stool.'

'What work'll I do, sir?'

'Living here will be your work. Living here for seven years. For the sake of knowledge, of science: to see how you fare without human society. Hermits choose to do it for *at least* seven years. Your name will become known.

'Keep it tidy, swept. There are brooms, everything you need of that nature. Wind the clock and mark off the days or you'll lose track of time. Read the books, Warlow. I've chosen them carefully.'

'Never read a book.'

'Yes, but you *can* read, can't you? And write. Write things down. There are pens, ink, paper and a journal. I'd keep a diary, if I were you. It would also be very useful to me when I write everything up to send to the Royal Society.'

'Journal, what's that, Mr Powyss, sir?'

'You write in it what you do each day. What happens. What you're thinking. It's a good thing you had *some* schooling.'

He shook his hand.

'Good luck, Warlow! Remember your wife and children are taken care of. You'll do it! We meet again in 1800.'

He smiled. Walked off in his fine black velvet breeches and coat.

Samuel nailed planks across the door.

Bed is soft and warm. No straw, no sacking. He's never slept in a bed like this. Could stay in it all day. *Is* it day? Clock strikes. He loses count. Utter darkness; the fire is out. No daylight.

He feels for the tinder-box, lights a candle. It's cold out of bed though he's still wearing his clothes. Pulls a blanket round him. Must find daylight. How else tell the time of day? Clocks are useless.

Takes the candle along the walls, floor, to corners, backwards and forwards. From one room to another. Starts again. Over the same ground. Along the walls, peering. Feeling with great rough fingers. Paper on walls near the fire. Plaster on others. Thick stone. Sudden cold air. Ventilation grating half-way down in a corner near the cistern. Curled ironwork flakes at his touch. Behind, a narrow brick-lined shaft that goes up out of sight.

A cut of light slants through. He breathes it. Smell of rust, leaf mould, morning.

*

Time is a stretch of toil. Eat. Another stretch. Plough half an acre of clay. Bread, beer. Plough another half. Horses back; brush them down. Home. Tiredness blotted by drink, bread, meat. Up again at daybreak.

Now there's no work. Nothing set. No compulsion. He's not tired. Not hungry. Meals descend. He rings the bell, hauls up scummy plates. His full pot in the morning. Days punctured by the dumb-waiter. Distant clatter the other side of the nailed door; muffled thumps way above.

Night's noise is children stirring, kicking, crying in the other bed, Hannah whimpering in her sleep, scratch of rats running overhead, dogs outside, owls. Now only ticking,

131

ticking. Nothing else. Nothing. He takes a kindling stick to the clock on the wall, opens the glass, jams it under the big hand. Which comes off. Can't read the time anyway. Tick, tick, tick. Unlatches a door in the side, reaches in. Heavy pendulum slips off its perch, crashes through the thin wooden base onto the floor. Tickticktickticktickticktickticktick. Stops.

His head ticks in the silence. *No*. That will make him mad. Stumbles to the grating to listen. To hear the life he's given up. Above, far away, a dog howls. Still coldness speaks of frost. Cracked crust of frozen earth. Roots alive beneath it. He is lower than turnips, potatoes. Lower than moles.

*

He's touched everything, handled, opened, closed, picked up, put down. Knows every damned thing here. Sits in the high-backed armchair, watches the candle burn down. Candlesticks, snuffer, oil lamp on the round table, cask of oil. Never used an oil lamp. Fiddles with it till it flares, melts an eyebrow, singes overhanging hair. He curses soundly. (Often talks to himself now.) Small Turkey rugs all swirling patterns, tongs, poker, shovel, brush, shelf of books, press with blankets, drawers of linen. Pictures of trees and lakes, people at a well: bible story, can't remember which. Stares into the looking-glass. Holds up the candle: a face recognisable only from the mouths it pulls at itself.

'Ohh. That . . . is me.'

The hand raised to feel the beard.

Powyss told him to write each day. He bites off tobacco, chews rapidly. Opens the journal, grasps a pen. His nails dig into his palm. He tears at them with his teeth. Dips the pen, writes his name.

John   Warlow

Tries to remember what they used to write in school: *I am 7.* Writes:

> *I am 4 3 yers old*   *I live in Moram Moream*
> *Morham   Moreham*
> *Febry 1793*

He knows the year, but days have passed, weeks. He crosses out *Febry* and writes *March.* Crosses that out, puts *Aperl.* He has no idea of the date though he hasn't yet smelled summer. That's enough for one go. His fingers are covered in ink; he's spilled sand all over the book.

He plunges his hand in the cistern and a frog jumps out, hops away into the dark. He bawls at it, spits, dries his fingers on his breeches, warms his arse before the fire.

Remembers what he said to Powyss. He'd be glad to be shut of human faces.

'For seven years, Warlow. To see nobody for seven years?'

'Yes.' Yes. Yes. He'd had no doubts.

It was the money. £50 wouldn't make him rich. But every year for the rest of his life! That was it. It'd keep the lot of them. He wouldn't work if he didn't feel like it. And if he did he'd keep his wages for himself. Drink as long as he wanted. Liberty. That was the word, wasn't it? Or was it freedom?

'For the rest of my life,' he murmurs over and over.

The others were envious you could see, though they said he was a fool.

But it was true about the faces. He'd rather look a horse in the face than see old Martin day after day, grimy dewlaps wobbling each time he took a swig. Dick grinning. Wind blew, they said, his mouth stuck. Sucking soaked crusts between his gums.

'No woman for seven year.'

He'll get by. There's no joy in Hannah. So scared of another child she'll do anything to avoid him. Scraping damned pans into the night, mending, scrubbing again and again. In the morning asleep at the table head on arms. She's had that many, eight living, five buried. Thin as a skeleton herself. He could kill her easy rolling on top. Her coughing, struggling for breath. The last time he hit her her arm broke. He hadn't done it since the girl was born.

Polly. He'll miss her. Her sweet look. But the rest. Good for nothing. Hungry all the time, fighting each other, he had to knock them about. Roars out loud at the thought of them. Can't tell one from the other. Sometimes calls them by the names of the ones who died. Dick says children are punishment.

*

Each day he goes to the grating to sniff the outside world. Soil, damp or dry. Knows when it's been raining; when spring begins to warm. When leaves on the other side, piling up in the brick-lined shaft are dusty with summer; when scores more gust in; rattle of ash-keys. Smoke-smell of fog; hears hail, soundless snowfall. And hooves on gravel, wheels, boys shouting, bells. Cocks, pigeons, rooks. All sounds shrunken, as from a tiny country.

It's through the rusting grating the frogs get in. He came across that first one, a flat, dried-out frog shape on the ground near the bed. Now he catches them, drops them in the cistern. Scatters crumbs, fragments of food on the surface.

It's when he smells hot earth that he longs to get out and shit among the leaves at the edge of the wood, chew bread with the others while sweating horses rest.

*

There's tapping. He's had his third meal so it must be evening. Strong dark meat he didn't recognise, boiled celery, plum dumpling. Pint of porter.

He scratches his scalp, the beard now down to his chest. Thinks he imagined it, but it's there all right. Other side of the nailed up door. He doesn't move. Mustn't reply. To get his reward he must speak to no one. Then it stops.

Is it Hannah? No. Powyss said he'd take care of them while he's below. And she'll not have anything to say. She'll be glad, very glad he isn't there.

Days later it happens again. He pushes hair from his eyes, presses his ear against the door. A woman's voice.

'Mr Warlow? John? I know you're there. Just the other side of the door.'

He presses harder, accidentally scratches the door with long nails.

'I can hear you're there.' He thrusts his fingers into his mouth, gnaws off the nails.

'I know you're there, John. You poor man.'

He's breathing hard. Mustn't reply. For so long now he's been saying his thoughts aloud, taking comfort from the sound of himself. Perhaps it's a trap. To make him speak, lose the money.

'John?'

A young voice. Who is she?

'It's Annie. I work in the kitchen.' He doesn't know her. But he never had to do with the house until all this. 'I know what you look like, John. What you *looked* like. You look different now, I reckon. I could tell you things, John.'

He groans to himself. Maybe it's the voice of the devil. Isn't that what they say? He speaks in the voice of an angel to tempt you. He moves away from the door. Behind the table as if to protect himself. Says the name of Jesus three times. Tiptoes back.

Then there's scuffling, a man's voice.

'Come away! Stupid girl!' He recognises Stephens. 'What are you thinking of? He's not allowed to speak.'

'It's cruel. Poor man! And his wife ...' Her words suddenly muffled as by a hand.

'He agreed to it. Didn't need to. He must abide there.' Shouted for his hearing. More scuffling. Silence.

For some time he is buoyed by this episode. The girl is thinking about him! She's kind. Young. Pretty no doubt. Ample. She'd need to be strong in the kitchen. He pictures her reddened by steam, meeting him in Horseshoe Copse. Eager. Greedy. He imagines.

For he'll be famous when he comes out. Powyss said so. He'll be a wonder. They'll all want him. And Hannah? Hannah will probably be dead by then. Yes, these thoughts buoy him up for days.

*

He can sense daylight. Knows he's right when he hears the first meal begin its downward journey. Gets up, greedy for bread. Or doesn't. They'll not wind the dishes up till he rings the bell. Can lie as long as he likes. Imagining Annie's breasts, buttocks. Eventually bladder compels.

Kidneys, lamb chops, white bread, butter, jam, the beer he asked for. Sits on the close-stool scratching back, groin, behind the knees, digging into the skin until it bleeds. Buttons himself, lifts the pot, rings for its shaky journey up to where he cannot go. Clean one descends.

At the grating he breathes heat or dripping cold. Confirms the world still exists. Grips the flaking iron, shakes it. If he loosened it what then? Too small to get through. Not think about getting out.

Checks traps. He has several, sent down when he wrote:

I ned rat trapps pleas 5

Builds a new fire, burns the corpses.

Tends to frogs. He tried putting them back between the curls of rusting iron but they can't jump high enough to get out of the chute. Once fallen they're stuck. Drawn to the cistern, lured to its lifeless water.

The futility of their life troubles him. When he finds one floating on its back he's depressed for days. Then he thinks to catch them, put them under a dish-cover, send them upstairs. He laughs to think of the women shrieking as frogs spring off the dish. But he won't have them killed.

pt froggs in pon   pleas

Now the long gap of morning. Once in a while he opens a book and flicks its pages as if this time it will make sense. Writes only when there's something to ask for. Chews. Spits. Sits. Stands by the nailed door. Distant kitchen sounds. Annie hasn't come back. Sits again. Scratches the webs of his fingers. Kicks off clogs, scratches the webs of his toes. If Annie's left she'll have no option. He thinks of Moreham men enjoying her.

His sight grows used to dimness, smell and hearing sharpen. As seasons pass he labours in his mind: mud, seed, weeds, grain. Herding, thwacking flanks, tugging warm udders. Plods up a furrow, down the next. But this occupies minutes only. Mind grinds down like a windless mill with no corn. Great stones, weighted, waiting.

He scratches his lice-thick hairiness. Curses. Thinks how to burn off some hair. That's not *cutting*, is it? But how can he do it without setting his head alight?

Feet hurt. He saws the nails with a knife. Powyss won't know: they'll grow again. But they're like horn. Tries forcing a foot up into his mouth but his body is thick and stiff with inactivity. Topples off the chair; lies on the patterned rug bemused. Why move? For what? Until he gets cold.

And when the meal comes creaking down it disgusts him. Pieces of soft fish hidden in thick, winey sauce. Unknown vegetables. Freezing ice-cream. Powyss somewhere above, eating the same. He scrapes it into the traps.

More blank hours. Fear runs across his mind like black beetles. He closes his eyes, dozes. Dreams prompt memory. They thought he was a fool. Are they right? Fifty pound. Fifty pound. He wants someone to tell him he was right to agree.

Mother was always old, working, never still until the end. Had no time for any of them. Hannah is already like her. His father was trampled, crushed by a bolting horse and cart. Then he and the rest scared crows, dug ditches, hauled branches for their keep until old enough to plough.

Only Mary looked at him without loathing or annoyance. With sweetness. His sister Mary. He refuses to think of her end. She, now. She'd tell him what's right.

*

One day he hears sounds above. Close. Realises they've always been there. All the years. *John Warlow   4 7 yers old.* Listens. Moves away from flames cracking in the grate. Listens. Silence for minutes. Someone, he's sure of it. Someone way above, listening. Listening to him listening.

Scraping sound. Then he knows they've gone.

Came from the ceiling. He takes the lamp, chair. Reaches up, feels with big hands, black now from no washing, dried scabs. Planks, beams. Cries out as a splinter jabs into his flesh.

Knot-hole. No. He puts two fingers in it. Feels metal. Sticks a broom handle into it. Way up.

Powyss listens through this hole! He made it to listen. Damned Powyss. Never *said*, did he! Listening all this time! Can he *see*? Is he *watching* him, too? Shove the broomstick in his eye!

Everything changes with this knowledge. Powyss could be listening at any time. So he fills the day with tasks. Clears out the ash, sweeps the hearth, brushes mats, writes in the journal, cleans out the traps, takes the books off the shelf, puts them in a pile, replaces them, opens one, holds the illustrations under the lamp to fathom the story. Raises the organ lid, pumps with his feet, plays a note, another, closes the lid.

Screws a piece of foolscap into a ball, rams it in the hole.

Later he finds it on the ground. Searches through the box of kindling. Finds thin sticks to jam in the hole, but they, too, are on the ground the next day.

Does Powyss know he knows or doesn't he? He dips the pen:

Mr Powis   I no yor lisnin

Sends it up with his soil pot.

 No reply.

'Damn Powyss! Damn! Shut me down here. Yes, I said yes. How did I know? It's prison! For science, he said. What's science? It mean no Freedom. No Freedom for likes of us.'

Remembered phrases bubble like gas.

'Them as has money does what they likes. Puts people in prison for science. Damn to Powyss! Damn to the government! Damn to the King!'

He paces about, shouting, relieved it all makes sense. Men painting on the market cross 'Liberty'. And that other word. He, here, is part of the great stirring that began before he came below. The great grumbling that grew in the taverns. Men shooting an effigy of somebody. He hopes Powyss can hear him.

He tires of bawling. But can't stop thinking of Powyss in his fine black velvet coat. Listening through the hole at every moment. Easy smiles. Proud. Of all this! Picks up, flings shovel and tongs down onto the hearth. What he'd do if only he could get upstairs! Give me an axe!

But wait. He's got fire. Can fire the house. Tonight when

Powyss has gone to bed, no longer above him. Stuff more paper through the hole. No, strips of linen. He's already ripped a shirt for a length to tie back his hair. Smear them thick with butter. Push all the way up. Light a taper. Blow bellows! It'll soon catch fire, then boards, carpets, furniture.

He knows men do it these days, pull down houses, fire them. He's heard. Bands of men; but he'll do it on his own. Praise in the village. Not the fool they said he was.

Flames, big flames, tall as houses, licking chimneys. He's seen it. Houses that burned in Moreham when he was a boy. Burning ember began it, they said. People and animals jumping out, screaming. Streams of rats and mice. Stood and watched in huddles. People counted. Only the end house when all had burned to nothing. Two bodies in the cellar.

'Aah. Aah!' Bangs the table with huge fists, head. 'Ah, how can I do it? Cannot get out. Must get out.' Howls. Overturns table. Glass shatters from pictures hurled. Howls. Ripped books shower their shreds.

'Pump with your feet!' Howls. Presses both arms hard on the keyboard: howling crowd of sounds, takes the chair to it, poker to the case, pulls out wood shards with his hands, bloody with cuts, crumples, falls exhausted. Sleeps.

*

Wakes to the creak of the dumb-waiter. A meal descends. Half a roast fowl, bacon, peas. A salad. Redcurrant tart. Pint of porter.

He kicks paths through the debris. From bed to close-stool to dumb-waiter. Most days he lies in bed wrapped in the smell of himself. Cares not for the outside world. Listens to mice back and forth beneath his bed, infernal buzzing of flies. Another summer passes. He is defeated.

Lying on his back in the dark he hears a distant shout

above. A high cry. Open window in the house.

Sleeping, waking, there is little difference. Dreaming of Mary. Mary coming towards him arms wide open, calling his name. In the dark after he'd scared crows all day from first light.

Is it morning? He lights the stump. Plates on the table. Congealed lamb's fry. Empty beer jug. His full pot on the dumb-waiter. He'd returned to bed, not rung the bell.

Suddenly he knows he wasn't asleep. Drags the table over, gasping for breath, places the chair on top of it under the hole. Kneels on the seat. Ear to the hole. Nothing. Something blocking. Climbs off. Smashes broom on the flags to break off the head. Climbs up again. Breathless. Pushes it in with another broom beneath to make it go further. Up, up. Something light shifts away. He stops panting. Slides the handles down. Listens.

'See to it, Stephens.'

'Yes, sir.'

A door closes. Silence.

He smiles, smiles at the reversal. Laughs. *He* will listen to *Powyss*.

He does it with diligence. No sound for ages. Powyss is solitary. Reads books for hours. He may wait for days. Sits contorted next to the ceiling. Hair sticky with cobweb. Sleeps at night with neck and shoulder aching. Returns to his cramped post each morning.

'Here we are again, Polly! Which flowers did you look at in the garden on your way here?'

'Big red daisy flowers, Mr Powyss. I likes them.'

The voices move away down the room. He hears tones not words. Still he listens, immobile. Polly his child. Baptised in remembrance of his sister Mary. Sweet face. His beard is wet with tears.

No Applause

Hogweed heads stand dry in late September fields; a spring-tide of goosegrass shrivels to crisp cobwebs. On the hot stone terrace cats bask. Prowl half-heartedly. Fitz stretches out, dozes, nose between huge forelegs.

She watches them. Stands at the window watching them and the sky: the subtle shift into a new season; the day's magnificent protest.

Here's Mitchell.

'Will you take your tea at the little table, your ladyship?'

'Yes of course I shall. You know perfectly well I shall want to see the sunset, Mitchell.'

Mitchell's as old as me. Looks dreadful, but she will frown so when she speaks. I know exactly what the woman's thinking, but I'm not changing now.

'Mitchell, when did Mrs Dent say she'd come next? She is supposed to bring me one of those new German songs. For Haydn is dead of course. And Handel a thing of the past.' She sighs.

When it's dusk she'll read. The new gaslight is a wonder. She's kept up with the times. Mrs Dent brings the latest novels. *She, too, looks at me as though to say 'if only you'd . . .'*

Here's Gerald.

'Lady Gatcombe, the carriage, your ladyship.'

'Yes, what of it?'

'It have dropped all to pieces. Will you not come and see with your own eyes, your ladyship?'

'Dropped to *pieces*? Why would it do that?'

'It have not been used these twenty year, your ladyship. It is eaten away.'

'Clear it out then, Gerald. Build a huge fire for the poor children in the village. There *are* still poor children in the village? I'll look out for the blaze from the upstairs drawing room. Col. Corbett can buy fireworks when next he goes to London. That will cheer everyone.'

A small disagreement with a servant is nothing. Servant resentment was a familiar at my birth. And Mrs Dent and Col. Corbett will never say what they think to my face. They live off the dregs of my reputation.

She drums the window frame in mild annoyance. The dog's ears prick up, he looks round. She smiles at him and he sleeps again.

Snubs. Rebuffs. Animals never snub you. Backbite. Vilify.

Fireworks make her think of violent death. Mrs Clitherow and her family in Half-Moon Alley, up all night stuffing paper tubes with fuses and gunpowder for November 5th. Burned to death, the whole lot of them, running in and out trying to save each other amid dazzling explosions and showers of brick.

And *that* always reminds her of her first marriage, for she saw the illumination, not yet knowing what it meant, standing outraged at the window of her bedroom. Harriet Sayles, 16, to the Revd. Mr J. Bone, 42. Her impoverished father, Sir Richard Sayles, relieved of the cost of her, her mother relieved of the responsibility, a girl already striking, headstrong, wayward. Mr Bone's furtive authority would keep her from straying, they thought. And he hated music.

Of course I ran away. And was found bemused in the street by Mrs Clavering on the look-out for new girls for her 'nunnery'. Powdered, perfumed, fashionably dressed, Mrs Clavering flattered her, smiling through steeliness, bought her clothes, took her several times to Jefferey's jeweller. Discovered and *adored* her singing voice, bought a harpsichord, briefly hired Vercelli, a singing master not attracted to women. The penury of Harriet's childhood was swept away in a month of apparently unrestrained spending.

But she was not malleable. She had shone at her girls' school in Chelsea, reaped incessant praise, expected listeners to attend to her and none else. What her mother took to be waywardness was confidence, determination, stubbornness. Mrs Clavering perceived that the girl had more education than she. Might strike her with a Latin tag. She met her match.

'I'll be no common harlot!'

'Why Harriet, no girl in my establishment is a *harlot*. Look at where we are,' she said in an unusually wheedling tone. 'Jermyn Street, just by St James's. Gentlemen who call here are the greatest in the land. They expect only the highest quality. Not merely are you beautiful. You have a voice they will long to hear.'

'I am willing to sing.'

'And make conversation too, Harriet.'

'By 'conversation' I mean speaking about poetry and music, Madam. There is to be no bed. My bedroom must be elsewhere.'

'Then you cannot have a special mattress.'

To Harriet the advantages of this arrangement were considerable. She was fed, clothed and groomed to a standard higher than she'd ever known, surrounded by handsome, expensive if somewhat miscellaneous furniture and paintings. The harpsichord was excellent and tuned daily. She slept alone.

And Mrs Clavering soon saw a return for her investment in Harriet's unorthodox behaviour. Although she was costly in trinkets and gowns she'd required no training, having excellent manners already. Her voice really was exquisite as was her haughtiness, so that Mrs Clavering's reputation rose magnificently in the firmament of the demi-monde. The more refined clients, often the grandest, paid well to listen and be disdained.

To prevent lascivious talk Harriet would on occasion read to them. Poetry, the tedious parts of novels, then, once, found lying under folders of lewd drawings, *The Rights of Man*. She chose passages with which to insult her listeners yet what did they do but revel in the castigation, licking up the words like cats with sly eyes.

'Oh! To watch those impertinent phrases drop from such lips! Listening to Harriet Sayles read the traitor Paine is better than a good whipping, by *far*,' said Lord M.

The sun has burned down with casual brilliance and she rests with her newly-cut novel brought by assiduous Mrs Dent, cats beside her, dog at her feet. She consumes novels like daily bread. Thus absorbed she can exclude memory.

Sometimes she sings. Late at night when the servants are in bed. For once, trying out her new fortepiano, there was applause outside the door. Her voice is not what it was.

I didn't just sing for the 'gentlemen'. I sang for myself. When the novelty of material advantage ceased she looked about her with dismay. She had no friends among the girls who regarded her arrangement as cheating, abhorred her superiority. However much Mrs Clavering claimed that her establishment in Jermyn Street was no different from any house within easy walking distance of the palace, Harriet could hardly help overhearing the evidence of Mrs Clavering's trade: squeals, groans, moans, hoots, roars, snores, running feet, lurching steps, thud of falling bodies.

She sang to drown the sounds around her. The more she heard the more she sang. Of love, death, longing, despair. Of hopeless loss and glorious adoration. She flooded her being with passion and ardour amidst the mêlée of tangling limbs, jangling coins, rattling pill boxes.

There was a fatal flaw in Mrs Clavering's plan: Harriet was never corrupted. She sang all day. *I cannot live alone without my love. My dearest woodlands, farewell. Ice and snow have finally melted. I feel within my heart such pain and sorrow. Lascia ch'io pianga. Figlia mia, non pianger, nò. Lasciate mi morire.*

She *was* Ariadne, Eurydice, Dido, Almirena.

And came to realise that the gulf between her sung life of wonderful suffering and the world of Jermyn Street was absurdly great. Somewhere, *surely* she could find love?

'I wish to leave,' she announced. Soon after, Mrs Clavering presented her with a bill for £1,354, 12 shillings for eighteen months' board, lodging, gowns, kerchiefs, ribbons, hairdressing. A further £500 for jewels or she must return them. Then told her the story of the girl who'd protested, whom she turned onto the street quite naked.

There was only one way to get out.

She'd had many offers, though few of marriage. Lord this, Lord that promised huge yearly allowances, a house in Grosvenor Square, clothes, diamond necklaces, her own carriage and liveried servants, such was their proclaimed Ardour and Passion.

In the end she accepted Gatcombe's offer of marriage. It was by no means the best, but he was a little younger, slightly less odious than the rest. It wasn't love of course. The gulf was not filled. He was certainly an improvement on Revd. Mr Bone (who, meanwhile, had conveniently died) for he liked a good tune, but his interests were not hers and his attention span was small.

There's no stopping memory now.

'No. Mitchell, I shall go to bed later tonight. I'll ring when I need you.'

She lifts a cat onto her lap, pats the sofa for Fitz to join her which the huge wolfhound does delicately, like a small horse. *Mitchell disapproving again.*

Gatcombe's family was old, his money evident enough if not overflowing, but neither was enough to counter obloquy. The marriage was an affront. No one *wanted* to approve of it. Harriet Sayles had been a demi-rep; marriage into one of the country's oldest families could not disguise a past at Mrs Clavering's. Gatcombe was a fool. She couldn't possibly be accepted by the best in society.

She sees herself at a ball approaching a battery of *grandes dames*, formidably coiffured. Fifty-four-gun women of war in formation. *What* did she say her name was? Pray, repeat it, would you? Greetings that barely slip through lips, tones of dismay, breaths sucked in disgust; fingers held out, limp with distaste; eyes sidling; sudden cessations of speech; her name caught muttered behind fans; sniggers, snubs, sneers, men's leers. *Morning Post*. Satires. Smears. Tide of retreating gowns.

He took her to Italy where surely no one would know. In golden Florence the British Envoy received her; in sunny, stinking Naples they barred the doors.

She rings the bell, hastens to bed. Counts out her drops, adds fifteen or twenty more and sleeps.

Next morning, brushing the thin strands, Mitchell says: 'Lady Gatcombe.'

'You're going to tell me off – I can hear it in your tone.' *See how she frowns at the back of my head. Look at my face now. Surely Harriet Sayles still glares with the same old fire?*

'No, my lady, certainly not. It's the Colonel. He has confided in me.'

'Goodness, Mitchell! Really?'

Mitchell knows her mistress is difficult in the morning.

'He has asked that you inspect his new spinet.'

Mitchell and Harriet Gatcombe see more of each other than most married couples. Mitchell's loyalty is faultless, her guile not at all.

'He told me there could be no better person to assess his new purchase and that he would send his carriage with curtains drawn.'

'*With curtains drawn*! Mitchell, how can you imagine that I do not see straight through your stratagems, your conspiracies with Colonel Corbett. *With curtains drawn*! I shouldn't do it if the entire carriage were shrouded in black crepe! I shall not do it. *You* know I shall not. Tell him all spinets are the same!'

They abandoned abroad. Gatcombe was surprised by their reception. Annoyed, for it touched his own reputation. Had he imagined that he could sweep all before him? Had he been too stupid to anticipate it? Considerate at first, his patience quickly fled and Lord and Lady Gatcombe returned to England where an old disease caught up with him at last.

She didn't miss him, except that there was no one to share humiliation. Her confidence was shot ragged by fleets of well-aimed cannon. Determination exploded amid showers of brickbats.

Only stubbornness remained.

Her house is fine, remote from the metropolis, the vistas from the windows pleasing, unpeopled. There's an income; she wants for nothing. Here she's safe. She has no expectations. The gulf was never bridged. Longing, love, grief remain hers to enjoy alone.

Each day she discusses the menu with the cook. She has become fat, her once glorious hair now thin and faded beneath its cap. Her life is dull but safety and certainty defeat loneliness. The servants are used to her, know what she wants. They only look at her that way out of habit.

I know what they say among themselves. If only she'd go out. It would do her good, they say. She hasn't left the house for twenty-three years.

Her breathing is poor. She refuses to be bled but summons a lawyer.

'Mr Bearcroft, I shall leave £20 a year for each cat, £25 for Fitz. Until their deaths.

'I leave £2000 each to Mitchell and Gerald. Oh and to Mrs Ramp, my cook. Mrs Dent can take as many of my novels as she likes and the Colonel. Hmm. Would it be cruel to leave him my fortepiano when he can hardly play?

'£1000 each year to provide loaves for the poor of the village. How many that will be per week I've no idea. Someone will have to do the sums.

'There's to be a special fund of £5,000 for poor girls of the district to keep them at home or in service nearby. It must be well invested. On no account are they to go to London.'

The streets of St James's surge through her memory and with them a realisation she faces suddenly for the first time.

I shall be taken out of the house! I have stayed indoors for twenty-three years but I shall be carried out! Of course I'll be dead, but all the same, they'll get me out at last; what they've wanted all this time, Mitchell, Dent, Corbett, Gerald.

And what if I'm not dead? What if they think I'm dead but I'm still alive?

'Take this down, Mr Bearcroft. There is to be no funeral until four weeks after my death.'

'But Lady Gatcombe . . . '

'No! Don't interrupt. So as not to become offensive, my body is to be washed each day in spirits. Mitchell can do that. Unless she's dead herself of course.

'Only then may my body be removed from the house. And in two coffins, the outer one of oak. These two will be encased in two more, the outer one of marble and placed in the Gatcombe vault.'

I shall not be disturbed. No sounds will penetrate the marble. No cavorting, moans, squeals will reach my ears. No remarks, titters, gasps at the sight of me. Nor shall I see eyebrows rise, mouths frown, nostrils flare; nothing ridiculous, mocking, no cruelty.

If corpses sing I'll charm myself with songs. No one will hear me. There'll be no applause.

Notes

His Last Fire

Cape St Vincent   Admirals Jervis and Nelson defeated the Spanish off Cape St Vincent in 1797

Opera house   This was the King's Theatre, Haymarket.

The Play's the Thing

London Corresponding Society   Consisted largely of artisans, small traders, clerks and labourers wanting reform of parliament and elections and manhood suffrage. Corresponded with similar societies throughout the country of which there were about 80. Very active in the 1790s, finally suppressed in 1799.

Catapotium   Purging pill, to be swallowed without chewing.

| *Fizz-gig* | Gadding, idle gossip. |
| *Cold-bath-fields* | House of Correction, Clerkenwell, built 1794. |

Flask Between the Lips

| *Brighthelmstone* | Brighton |
| *Memoirs* | *Memoirs of the Late Mrs Robinson Written by Herself.* This was Mary 'Perdita' Robinson, actress, writer, notorious beauty. |

Revolutionary

Copemen	Receivers of stolen goods.
Light-horsemen	Renegade mates of ships and revenue officers.
Scuffle-hunters	Thieves of goods from quaysides.
Tom Paine	His *Rights of Man vol. I*, price 3/-, sold 50,000 copies in 1791. By 1793, after *vol. II* had been published in 1792, 200,000 copies had been sold. Paine fled to France, was prosecuted in his absence, and *Rights of Man* banned as seditious libel.

SHELL: THE PEDLAR'S TALE

Gordon Riots   In June 1780 the delivery of an
            Anti-Catholic petition to Parliament
            by the Protestant Association, led by
            Lord George Gordon, drew huge
            crowds which turned riotous.
            Enormous destruction over several
            days ravaged London; the army was
            called in; 285 rioters were killed.

Coram's   Foundling hospital built mid-century
            in Lamb's Conduit Fields.

SHELL: THE SAILOR'S TALE

Victory   Admiral Duncan defeated the Dutch
            at Camperdown, October 1797.

Quota-men Those who took money to join the
            navy. Usually prisoners.

Mutiny   From April-June, 1797, the fleet
            mutinied at Nore and Spithead.

LASCIA CH'IO PIANGA

A Two-decker Firing   Oil painting by Lieutenant Thomas
a Morning Gun   Yates, 1790.

Burin   Engraving tool that cuts directly
            into metal plate, producing a line

which tapers to a point.

Lascia ch'io Pianga   Aria from Handel's *Rinaldo* (first
performed King's Theatre, 1711).

FORGIVEN

Foxite   Follower of Charles James Fox,
reformist politician, 'champion of the
People'. Foxite colours, buff and blue,
were copied from George
Washington's troops.

Thelwall   John Thelwall, Jacobin, friend of
Coleridge. His public lectures drew
huge numbers.

SHRIVEN

D'Oyley and Mant   The Authorized Version prepared
and arranged by The Revd. George
D'Oyley BD and The Revd. Richard
Mant DD, 1817.

FROM THE LIFE

Star-wheel   Four large spokes in wheel
formation to turn rollers of printing
press.

ACKNOWLEDGEMENTS

Thanks are due to the editors of *The London Magazine* for publishing 'His Last Fire' and an earlier version of 'The Play's the Thing'; *Penpusher* for an earlier version of 'Flask Between the Lips'; *New Welsh Review* for 'Forgiven' and *Ambit* for 'Eels' and 'Mad'.

To follow in March 2015...

The Flight of Sarah Battle

Alix Nathan

Born in her father's coffee house in Exchange Alley, London, Sarah Battle is brought up in an alcohol and smoke-thick atmosphere. Witnessing and suffering from the destruction of the Gordon Riots in 1780, she longs to escape her surroundings into a better life.

Her first attempt is via marriage to a man who's not what she thinks he is. Her second sees her in the brave new democratic world of late 1790s Philadelphia where she experiences deep love, warm friendship. On her final journey, exhilarating, dangerous, Sarah's vision of both past and future reveals the direction of a new life.

The Flight of Sarah Battle is set in the turbulent final decade of the 18th century in a London of rioters and revolutionaries hoping for a French invasion, and Philadelphia, bursting with new building and hope, with a democracy not quite fully fledged and shadowed by the terrible threat of yellow fever.

ISBN 978-1-909844-67-4
Paperback, £12.00

www.parthianbooks.com

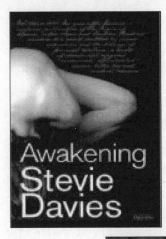

Awakening
Stevie
Davies

THE
VISITOR
KATHERINE
STANSFIELD

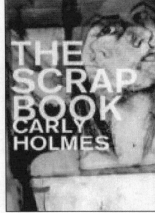

THE
SCRAP
BOOK
CARLY
HOLMES

PARTHIAN

NEW
FICTION

Dream On
Dai Smith

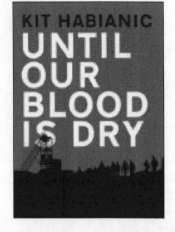

KIT HABIANIC
UNTIL
OUR
BLOOD
IS DRY